THE DEVIL'S QUILL

A Quartet of Halloween Stories

THE DEVIL'S QUILL

A Quartet of Halloween Stories

By

Andrew Charles Lark   Donald Levin

Whistlebox Press

Poison Toe Press

ISBN: 979-8-9877929-2-6

Cover photographs: Andrew Charles Lark
Cover design: Donald Levin

First edition published 2025

Printed in the United States of America

Contents

Foreword

I love being scared.

I have always felt that horror was an underrated genre—a genre that never gets the respect it deserves. But now I feel that horror is becoming a more mainline vein to our most sensitive places: our emotions and our society. Horror holds things that scare us. For those that eschew it, maybe it comes a bit(e) too close!

To read horror is to invite the vampire through the threshold—to open your mind, soul and dreams, that other place of mystery—to that very place that makes us unsure, terrified, and alone. It is the mental exercise of dancing with the very things we try every day to avoid; like death, losing loved ones, and even those things that could be worse than death.

And then, of course, besides the stories themselves, what could be lurking in the minds of the people who write horror stories? Those who say the names of the beasts out loud, and conjure them?

We are all afraid. Culturally speaking, every corner of the world has their monsters, demons, and ghosts. We all deal with our lives, deaths, and fears through storytelling, which of course helps to build culture in the first place. We walk through life in our suits with our schedules and our cell phones and our really important (mundane) work, but when we're in our rooms alone at night, curled up with our books, reading by that lone, dim light on the nightstand, we're inviting the nightmare to take us on that gallop toward the unknown. We even kick it on, facing death as our hearts beat louder and faster in defiance of it.

Who are the monsters in our worlds? We tell ourselves that they don't really exist, and that we make them up. But is it any better knowing that we create them? Or worse—that we enable them? We are obsessed with true crime, we rubberneck at car accidents, and we even vote horrors into high political office. The world is glued to the news where we listen to and watch every macabre detail—who blows up whom? Yet another serial killer with a catchy name is out there hunting victims. What new disease is causing mass death and altering our DNA? The reliance of dark-age-style religions and cults, the distrust of our fellow countrymen, the slaughter of innocents in the public square by mass killers; it reads as if I'm talking about home sweet home, but in actuality, it's plugged into the WWZ—the Worldwide Zeitgeist! Killers, vampires, werewolves, antichrists and zombies. We are all Dr. Frankensteins engaged in chasing our sins toward and into the icy floes of our subconscious.

What interests me most is how the stories end. Harkening to the basic morality offered by the Old Testament (talk about the slaughter of the innocents, turning people into salt, the destruction of humanity, cults, parents attempting to kill their children), the Brothers Grimm fairytales from the early 19th century, the atomic age horrors of Godzilla, aliens, and all those monsters—a reaction to nuclear fallout. Horror reprimands us by saying that we have more technology than intelligence, and not enough maturity to keep up and leash it.

Later came the teen slasher films that frankly I cut my fangs on. The most interesting part wasn't the imaginative (or unimaginative) slaughters themselves, but the killer that kept coming back. Death was not a barrier for the truly evil—the emotionless evil—the Mike Myers and Jason Voorhees—they weren't killing for revenge. They weren't killing for fun. They simply killed. They were emotionless killing machines in what amounted to a morality (and mortality?) tale on teenage promiscuity, drinking, and drug consumption. But what was in those endings? With a bogeyman you couldn't destroy, and a lone, emotionally wounded virgin—the sole-survivor of the ultimate penetration and "death"? *What was in the zeitgeist?* And what does it reveal about ourselves, the way we view people, our social norms, and those things that threaten them?

Do these horror tropes strive to simply entertain? Or do they allow us to practice facing what scares us most? Perhaps they're teachers that use terror to guide us toward morality?

Which brings me to the challenge given to lovers of horror in all its forms: what do our modern stories, like those in this anthology, say about us? The monsters are real.

How will *our* stories end?

Sara Cate Wolf

THE SHORT, UNHAPPY LIFE OF RUDY PEPPERS

Donald Levin

Vengeance is in my heart, death in my hand,
Blood and revenge are hammering in my head.
--Shakespeare, Titus Andronicus

1

On the street outside, a car alarm rang shrilly. It howled for five minutes, then abruptly went silent. The sounds of happy voices replaced it. Men and women and children's voices, loud, cheerful, resolving into laughter.

He saw the lower halves of the neighborhood children's Halloween costumes passing the window—the blue leggings and red boots of Spiderman outfits, teal gowns of Princess Elsas, yellow capes and goggles of Minions, and countless other costumes Rudy Peppers couldn't even identify. Not that he had any interest in what was happening in the world outside… Rudy lived in the basement apartment of his mother's house in Astoria, Queens, and cared not at all for events either at street level or in the wider culture. Sometimes, if he heard people outside and had nothing better to do, he looked up to see the legs passing on the other side of the grated windows in his living room. But tonight, the voices didn't interest him.

All he concentrated on were the thoughts he sent out and the movements he incited.

They went out through his headgear, a jerry-rigged affair of electrodes and circuits connecting his forehead to transistors on the Bell bicycle helmet he had scavenged from the trash on the next block and now wore atop his ratty hair. A visor extended over his face. The electrodes linked to leads that snaked down to earphones and from there to his mother's old blood pressure cuff wrapped around his right arm, connected in turn to the glowing innards of an outmoded CB radio from Best Buy, and from there on to a battered walkie-talkie. He had radically retrofitted the gear as a neurotransmitter and audio-visual receiver. At last his college degree in cybernetics was paying off in something other than wage-slavery.

Rudy sat in a crap-colored armchair with twin joysticks duct-taped to each tattered arm of the chair. At his feet, he had taped pedals to a board attached to the bottom of his chair. He worked the pedals as though shifting gears from foot to foot, and maneuvered the joysticks in a complex yet strangely delicate dance.

Overhead the floorboards creaked as his mother prepared their nightly hot cocoa. He tried not to think about her (she was prohibited from coming downstairs at any time; it was humiliating enough to live in his mother's basement at the age of thirty-five without her making cocoa for him every night, too), but kept his attention firmly on the matter at hand. When the drink was ready, she would leave his steaming cup for him at the top of the stairs, and he would take it whenever he wanted.

Many nights, like tonight, he was otherwise engaged and left the cocoa to grow cold; too much else was going on.

Tonight, however, she knocked on the door to the basement and called down: "Rudy, honey, don't you want to see the children in their Halloween costumes? They're so cute! You can help me give out the candy."

"No," he shouted back, "I told you a million times — don't disturb me when I'm working down here. And I'm *always* working!"

After a few moments, her feelings probably hurt, Rudy heard the sound of the basement door closing and her sad footsteps retreating across the ceiling.

"Stupid fucking cow," he muttered.

2

When the applause subsided, Leonard Curtis looked out over the waiting crowd. Several hundred people were present this evening in the ballroom of the Waldorf Astoria Hotel. Dressed in black tie, they were members of the New York City chapter of the American Lung Association gathered to see Leonard, the organization's Development Director, present the annual award for advancing the association's work. The ballroom was decorated with elegant black crepe bats hanging from the ceiling and swinging gently in wafts of air from the ventilation system, and fat crepe spiders dressed in tuxes squatting as centerpieces on all the tables.

Leonard cleared his throat and began. "Good evening, and thanks to you all for joining us on this, the 'scariest night of the year.' It is my great privilege to share the podium tonight with our honored guest." He leaned the top of his head toward the woman who sat immediately to his right on the dais. She gave a humble smile and ducked her head in appreciation.

"By any measure," Leonard continued, "Miriam Taylor is a national treasure. In her short career, she has already published over a hundred science fiction stories, a baker's dozen horror novels, ten nonfiction books, and three screenplays. Her work has been awarded the Bram Stoker Award, the World Horror Convention Grand Master Award, the Hugo, the Nebula, and the Edgar. She has had an asteroid named after her. She has consulted on motion pictures and television shows. And—I hope I'm not ungallantly betraying any secrets—all this before the age of forty."

He paused, and a spontaneous round of applause filled the silence.

When it faded, Leonard continued. "I'm not sure where she gets all the energy to be so productive. But 'I'll have what she's having.'"

The reference to a famous line from an old movie set off a smattering of polite laughter. For his part, Leonard kept a perfectly straight face.

"But more seriously," he went on, "tonight we are honoring her with the Stephen C. Joseph Award for Contributions to Pulmonary Health not simply for her literary accomplishments in general, but for one in particular: Dr. Taylor's book, *Smokescreen: The Nation's Health as a National Security Issue*, not only reached number two on the *New York Times* bestseller list, but also was responsible for changing the national conversation on cigarette smoking. Now, for the first time, we are able to see tobacco in the same context as the climate crisis, as a threat to our national existence. That is no small feat, and it is for that we honor Miriam Taylor tonight.

"Ladies and gentlemen, I am proud to present the Stephen C. Joseph Award to Dr. Miriam Taylor."

This time the applause was overwhelming as she stood to accept the crystal objet d'art. The ovation lasted several minutes before she could begin to speak.

3

Rudy Pepper's living space took up the entire tiny basement in his mother's house. His bed, an unmade mess, stood against the far wall next to the boiler, and a damp bathroom with toilet, sink, and shower had been shoe-horned into the opposite wall beside the hot water tank. He kept a hotplate and dorm-sized refrigerator next to the bathroom. By far the biggest pieces of furniture were his armchair and a wooden door lying horizontally across two sawhorses for use as a desk. Crowding the surface of the door was an assortment of electronics equipment with glowing red and green lights and the constant muted hum of a dozen small fans in each piece of equipment.

Rudy sat motionless in the chair. Anyone looking at the scrawny figure in filthy tee shirt and tattered jeans would have thought he was asleep. True, he was silent and still and his eyes were closed, but the spreading reptilian smile on his face would have given away the fact that he was conscious and alert. And very happy—not a typical state for the perpetually angry Rudy.

But then no one would have been down in his dank apartment to see him. He had no friends. On those occasions when he did venture outside for his shifts at the Best Buy where he worked in the repair department during the day (he had his own entrance leading into the garage attached to the house at home, so he didn't have to worry about his mother tracking his movements), he avoided all unnecessary human contact and therefore never invited anyone to visit his subterranean burrow.

His quarters were bare of any decoration except for his doodles scattered around the walls. No doubt they would distress his aged parent if she were allowed to see them. They were shockingly obscene scrawled pictures of men's and women's exaggerated genitals in every manner of proximity, with equally graphic (and bizarre) captions ("Blondes are brunettes, by cracky"). Rudy had gotten into the habit of making these drawings when he was a lonely and miserable college student. He was painfully, pathologically shy by nature, a loner possessing no social skills to speak of. Whenever he screwed his courage up to ask some cute girl or other out for coffee or a movie, he would inevitably get as reply some version of, "With who—you? Ew. No way. Who *are* you?"

A lonely and miserable adult, underemployed and alone in his widowed mother's basement, he still had the figures in his drawings as his closest companions.

Until now.

He now had someone whom he referred to as his Special Friend. It was definitely the closest human contact Rudy had ever had, even counting his mother.

And tonight, he reflected as he came alive, waggled his joysticks, worked his foot pedals, and sent his commands streaming through the ether, he and his Special Friend were taking care of business.

4

"Thank you, Leonard," Miriam Taylor began. She held up the award so all could see it. "I accept this lovely award with great humility."

She placed it on the podium and looked out across the faces in the crowd. "To my way of thinking, the work you are all doing to promote healthy living is among the most important work being done anywhere today. And I salute you all for your dedication."

She paused and coughed into her fist. Leonard Curtis was up in a flash with a glass of water for her. She nodded her thanks, took a drink, and went on.

"I say 'among' the most important work because, as significant as your efforts are, I think we all know there is a scourge today that affects all women. I refer, of course, to the serial killer stalking women in the borough of Manhattan, the one the newspapers are calling the Ghoul. As I was thinking about what to say this evening, I kept coming back to that. For as much as we all work hard to stop the merchants of death who sell cigarettes to our youth, and halt the spread of new strains of antibiotic resistant tuberculosis among the poorest citizens of our society, and contain the pollution that poisons our lungs—all that means little if New York City women don't have the freedom to feel safe in their own neighborhoods.

"The police have assured us they're doing everything they can, but so far, they've been ineffective. It really is up to us to look out for each other's safety. Today in New York City, more than at any other time in my memory, the possibility of sudden death for women is everywhere."

She let that statement hang in the air. During the past year, twelve women had been found dead in back alleys around the city, one every month, from the tip of Inwood Heights to the Staten Island ferry docks at the foot of Manhattan. They were all around the same age, in their thirties, all attractive and well-liked. Each had had sexual relations before being strangled, but as the months wore on, the level of brutality against them increased to the point where the last woman couldn't be identified because of the violence done to her face and hands. The clueless police had appealed to the public countless times for assistance. No one seemed to have any idea who was killing the women. The newspapers dubbed the killer the Halloween Ghoul since his first victim was found on Halloween and had been made-up with ghastly clown makeup—a wildly exaggerated smile, a nose reddened by lipstick, and a face deathly white from face powder. It was a practice that continued with every victim, no matter the race. As the killings continued, the media dropped "Halloween" from their moniker.

"Okay, then," Miriam said, "now that I have that out of my system, let's talk about pulmonary wellness as key to our nation's security. With the administration in Washington, we finally have a governmental partner sympathetic to our concerns."

5

Finding his Special Friend had turned out to be a complicated process. Rudy generally left the house only to go to work. Even when he did go out, he found it hard to break through the shell that seemed to have kept him separate from other people throughout his entire life. On the subway he never met another person's eyes, and at Best Buy he never spoke more than was necessary, sometimes simply writing down the serial numbers of the equipment he needed for his repairs and passing the note to the store clerks so he wouldn't have to talk to them at all.

When he was younger it ate at him, the way people—and women in particular—ignored him or else regarded him with cruel disdain, not appreciating who he was or how much he knew, or what his capabilities really were. Now he had developed a bottomless contempt for *everyone* he met, men as well as women and children. And soon he would show them all.

In order to make his plan work, however, he needed an accomplice. To find one, he hit on a strategy that was, he believed, inspired. The first step had been putting a personal ad in the back of the *Village Voice* and in online dating apps, pulling an online photo of a gorgeous anonymous blonde to accompany the ads:

Very attractive, charming, intelligent, independently wealthy 30ish woman desires serious, passionate LTR with kind professional man.

He received three dozen responses within the first two weeks. Using a false account that he had set up in a woman's name, he got in touch with all of the men who responded to his ad, and carried on an exchange of emails with each applicant. After he winnowed down the possibilities to a half dozen, he set up dates with the candidates. He would sit quietly in the coffee shops pretending to read when the hopeful men came to meet the woman of their dreams. The men waited for varying amounts of time, and then left after deciding they had been stood up.

After Rudy vetted several of them, one emerged as the best possibility. He seemed perfect: tall, strong-looking, handsome, expensively dressed, and supremely confident in his carriage. No children or family, according to Rudy's investigative work. He was everything Rudy was not. *Yes*, Rudy thought, trailing after the man through the dark city streets to his apartment on the upper east side of Manhattan, *you'll do just fine.*

Pleased to meet you, my Special Friend.

6

Her speech over, Miriam Taylor took a half hour of questions from the audience. When she answered the last question, Leonard Curtis stood up, thanked everyone for coming, and wished them all Happy Halloween. She was immediately mobbed by people wanting her to sign their copies of her books. She graciously agreed, which took another forty-five minutes.

By then, the banquet room had emptied except for Leonard and Miriam and the hotel staff cleaning up. "Some night!" he exclaimed.

"Yeah, this was a fabulous crowd. I had a great time."

"Thanks so much for coming."

"My pleasure."

As though taking that as his clue, Leonard leaned close to her. "The night doesn't have to end yet, does it?"

"Excuse me?"

"I'm just saying, it's still early. The shank of the evening, as they say. Fancy a nightcap? There's a great little bistro down in the Village that serves a Mojito to die for. And Halloween night in Greenwich Village is a rare experience."

She looked at him, sizing him up. He was a nice-looking man, it was true, with distinguished graying hair and fine strong bones in his face. He was younger than she was, but she did find some younger men attractive. And yet... there was something about him that put her off. Maybe it was his seriousness—he never cracked a smile all night. Or maybe the cologne. She hated men who wore cologne that preceded them into a room and lingered after they left, and this guy's was particularly putrid, with an intense musky smell that gave her a headache.

"Thanks," she said finally, "but I'm really beat. And I'm starting a book tour next week and I've got a million things to get ready. So I'm going to have to pass." She stuck out her hand. "Thanks for a great evening, though."

He took her hand and gave it a shake. "Maybe another time." He held on for a second too long. She found herself pulling away, stifling the urge to back away from him as far as she could.

She coughed again.

"One for the road?" he asked with a grin. He turned away to fetch her another glass of water.

7

Rudy had emailed the man he chose with a phony excuse for not meeting him:

> *I'm so sorry! My mother fell and broke her hip, and I wound up in the hospital with her for most of the night. In all the commotion, I didn't get the chance to message you. Can I make it up to you?*

The man emailed back that he was going on vacation for a few weeks, but he thought he might be able to squeeze in a quick dinner the next night. Better and better, Rudy thought.

He set up another meeting with the man, this time at one of the fancy French restaurants in midtown. Rudy stood in the shadows of a doorway down the street watching the man go in and then, a half-hour later, rush out, his face twisted in fury at having been stood up a second time. Rudy stepped out and followed in the man's wake. The man walked fast, radiating annoyance.

Ensuring they were alone on the sidewalk, Rudy came up behind him and plunged a syringe through the man's coat and into his back between his shoulder blades. The man lurched forward and Rudy got an arm around him to keep him upright long enough to steer him to the nearby alley where he left his mother's beater of a Chevy. Anyone seeing them would have thought one friend was just trying to help his drunk buddy stay upright.

By the time he got the man stuffed into the back seat, the sedative had taken complete effect and he was out cold. His heavy snoring punctuated the drive all the way back to Astoria.

Rudy parked his mother's car in the garage and struggled to get the man's dead weight into his basement apartment. It wasn't easy; the guy was large and heavy, and Rudy himself was thin to the point of emaciation. But he was determined, and through a combination of pushing and pulling and rolling he got the man into the middle of the floor of his apartment. He had planned to perform the procedure on his bed, but as he sat trying to catch his breath beside the large figure on the floor, Rudy decided he was fine just where he was.

When his breathing returned to normal, Rudy retrieved his equipment from his cluttered desk and began.

8

Miriam Taylor asked a doorman at the Waldorf to whistle her a cab, and as she stepped into the dirty vehicle she realized how exhausted she was. What she had told Leonard Curtis was the truth: she did have a national book tour to prepare for, and every night this week she had been busy. Tonight was the Lung Association, last night was the American Publishers Guild, the night before that a get-together for friends who were leaving on a world cruise... tonight she needed some downtime.

Not that Leonard Curtis was her type, under the best of circumstances. Well, okay, he was a handsome man, she'd give him that, but he was smarmy and slick, she reflected as the cab bore her across town. Something about him gave her the creeps. No, she was not lonely enough to take up his offer. Fortunately, he had the grace not to make a scene about it.

She sat back in the cab and began to think about all she had to do before she flew out on her tour—people to call, arrangements to make… her head began to whirl. She yawned. So tired... when she got back to her apartment, maybe she would just call it a night and wake up early to start her travel preparations in the morning.

She closed her eyes momentarily, just to rest them, and before she knew it she had fallen into a deep sleep.

She did not feel the hands lifting her out of the cab in front of her apartment building, nor did she hear a man tell the cabbie, "Oh, my, looks like she's had too much to drink again. When will she ever learn? Here, I'll get the fare."

Nor did she feel herself being carried into the man's beater of a Chevy and dumped into the back seat, nor the car crawling through the city's side streets. In fact, only when the man loomed over her and she smelled the heavy, musky cologne did she finally come to and realize what was happening.

9

The operation had gone as smoothly as Rudy had planned. Really, there wasn't much to it, just a small incision in the skin behind his ear and the insertion of the microchip within a pocket created in his skull. A few sutures and his new Special Friend was good to go.

In a few hours, the man on the floor began to groan. Rudy was ready for him. He was already sitting in his chair—his command center—with his Bell bicycle helmet with visor on his head and the electrodes attached to his forehead and arms, and his hands wrapped around the joysticks taped to the chair. He gave the right joystick a tentative wiggle, and could barely contain himself when the man lifted his right arm and made a throw-away gesture matching the instruction transmitted.

This, thought Rudy Peppers, is going to be great.

Because the man was supposed to be on vacation for the next three weeks, no one locally missed him as Rudy spent the time practicing with him. Keeping the man isolated and sedated in his basement lair, fine-tuning his method, Rudy discovered how to carefully modulate the controls so that he could bring the man in and out of consciousness, and gradually learned how to back off entirely while having perfectly reasonable conversations with the man one minute, then taking over his mind and body the next and having him perform any physical function Rudy wished. He made the man touch his toes; he made him lift the chair Rudy was sitting in; he made him stand on his head and recite the pledge of allegiance.

The best part was, the man didn't seem to remember what Rudy made him do, or indeed know that anything was out of the ordinary. Rudy had successfully taken over his entire neural processing system. With one exception: The only thing Rudy couldn't get him to do was smile; some gap in the circuitry wouldn't let Rudy control anything to do with emotions.

No matter. Emotions only complicated matters anyway. Together they began to form a coherent symbiotic relationship, in perfect harmony through the mediation of Rudy's technology. It was as though each had been waiting for the other to complete him. It got to the point where Rudy could bring his Special Friend under control with just the touch of a button on the walkie talkie connected to his rig.

Near the end of the three weeks, Rudy was adept enough at manipulating the man to try a dry run. Rudy had his Special Friend drive back to the city in the old Chevy. The man parked around the corner from a bar in Soho, then strolled into the bar, every movement controlled from Astoria. Rudy saw and heard everything the man could, even tasting the stale beer as the man sat at the bar chatting up the barmaid. She was a knockout brunette with a delightful Irish brogue and short, pixyish hair and dressed entirely in a black leotard. Her name badge read *Fiona*. She was exactly the kind of woman who would never give Rudy a second look, who would make him feel inadequate and useless just because she could. Exactly the kind who had made him miserable all his life.

This was as far as Rudy dared to go for the first outing. He recalled the man back to the basement apartment.

The next night—Halloween, as it happened, entirely appropriately—Rudy felt everything was ready. He sent his Special Friend back to the bar at closing time. Without going in, the Friend lingered outside the front door, with Rudy directing his every move through his joysticks, foot pedals, and mental connections. When at the end of her shift Fiona passed by in her Halloween costume of a fluffy cat tail and two perky cat ears, Rudy had his Special Friend step from the shadows and "accidently" bump into her. He invited her out for a drink.

"Oh," she said, "well, I'd love to, except this has been a long day—I really need to get home and sleep."

"Ah, come on," Rudy had him reply, "remember what Ben Franklin said: you'll have plenty of time to sleep when you're dead."

10

In the darkness, his eyes were as black and lifeless as two marbles. His face floated six inches above Miriam Taylor's as she lay on the musty back seat, his full weight pressing her into the springs. She could feel his insistent erection against her. He was not breathing hard, the rational portion of her mind noticed as she fought to control her fear. He seemed no more excited than he had been behind the podium back at the Waldorf ballroom less than an hour ago.

"What—what are you doing, Leonard?" she forced herself to ask. She would not show him the panic that tried to force itself into her throat from her wildly beating heart.

When he didn't answer, she tried to move her legs but Leonard Curtis had them pinned with his knee. "What are you doing?" she demanded again.

"Isn't it obvious?" He replied calmly, even intimately. He moved both her arms over her head and produced a long thin blade. He pressed it under the point of her chin until he drew blood. "I'm getting ready to slice pieces out of you. And then I'm going to kill you."

11

Rudy wanted the first time to be in his basement apartment so he could oversee events first-hand.

Under Rudy's skillful manipulations, and hiding where the barmaid couldn't see him, the fun started when Fiona and Leonard slowly removed each other's clothing. Rudy had his Special Friend pull her leggings down and spread her legs, something he had never done to a woman on his own. Fiona lay on the bed, and Leonard pounded inside her like angry surf. She called for more, and Rudy had a hard time keeping up with her demands. This is what real sex was like—except his Special Friend's lack of emotion transferred back to Rudy… try as he might, he couldn't muster any excitement besides the raw physical sensations that made him feel like jumping out of his skin.

Otherwise, Leonard performed perfectly, rolling off the woozy barmaid when he finished. They kissed. Leonard said, "Hey, don't forget—tonight's Halloween. Wanna wear a mask?"

Leonard took makeup from her purse and painted her face as a grotesque clown with a red lipstick nose and exaggerated lipstick smile.

She took her makeup and began to paint Leonard's face, and that's when Rudy—frantic because the whole experience left him still frozen inside, a vast, iced-over lake—decided he had had enough.

He made Leonard's large hands settle around the barmaid's throat in perfect congruence with Rudy's toggling on the joysticks.

From his hiding place, watching the man standing over Fiona kicking and bucking ever more slowly as he choked the life out of her, Rudy realized it was too dangerous to have these things happening in his mother's home. From now on, he would have to be careful to make the encounters take place in some distant part of the city.

As a remembrance, he kept Fiona's waitress name badge (*Hi! I'm Fiona*) in a box in the nightstand beside his bed.

So began Rudy Peppers's reign of terror over the women of Manhattan. It would continue for the next year. Every month, under Rudy's control, Leonard Curtis first seduced a woman and then made her pay with her life for her gender's spiteful mistreatment of Rudy. There was the salesclerk at Saks, the human resources director at Columbia-Presbyterian Medical Center, the English professor at NYU, the secretary at Time-Life, a midtown real estate agent, and so many more… with every death, as Rudy amped up the violence, the city grew more fearful. And always he had his Special Friend leave their faces painted as disturbingly happy clowns.

For the first time in his life, Rudy Peppers was happy.

12

Was she having a Halloween nightmare? Was she still back in the cab, dreaming? Why was this happening?

"Leonard, please, why are you doing this? I don't understand."

"You don't need to understand," Leonard murmured as though to a lover. "All you have to do is die."

He moved the knife from under her chin and drew it lovingly down the length of her smooth cheek. Blood bloomed under the blade.

When she felt his muscles grows stiff and he froze as though someone had hit pause, she thought, *Not today, pal,* and summoning every bit of strength, she edged her right leg underneath his heavy body and drove her knee into his groin.

He howled in rage and pain and shoved the knife into her gut.

Rudy let up on the joysticks back in Astoria in the transmitted shock and agony of her knee to his balls. In the shifting of Leonard's weight, Miriam freed her hands from his grip and raked her nails across his face. Red welts formed angry diagonals from his eyebrows across his nose to his chin. He rose up screaming—Rudy in Queens doing the same—and she pulled the knife from where he stabbed her and plunged it into his neck.

The blood spray momentarily blinded her but she landed another knee between his legs and succeeded in pushing him completely away from her. Freed of his weight, she scrambled out the back door of the Chevy, screaming for help.

One hand holding the wound in his throat, Leonard Curtis made a desperate grab for her but missed. She continued shouting for help as she tried to scuttle away from the car on her hands and knees. Naked, mortally wounded, she didn't get far before her arms and legs gave out and she hit the sidewalk face-first.

Back in his basement, in pain, confused, unsure how things had gotten so completely out of hand, Rudy regained control over his Special Friend—now deader weight than ever, bleeding out from his neck wound—and made him flop behind the wheel of the Chevy. He peeled out of the alley where he had parked, leaving Miriam Taylor behind.

13

The dead man pulled into the garage in Astoria and stumbled into Rudy's apartment. His face was raw from Miriam's fingernails. The blood from the neck wound drenched his clothes. Rudy let him collapse on the floor.

He gazed down at the man in total disbelief. This was the first time any of the women had put up a fight. Usually they were no match for Leonard Curtis's strength or Rudy's wiles.

This was bad.

The first orders of business were getting rid of both this useless hulk on his floor and the Chevy, which must have been blood-soaked beyond recovery. Rudy wrapped Leonard in a raincoat to cover his bloody clothes and a scarf to hide the neck wound. Next, he reconnected himself to his mind-control rig. He made Leonard sit up and go into the garage and drive the Chevy down Ditmars Boulevard to the nearby East River. He abandoned the Chevy near Astoria Park (Rudy assumed the car would be stripped for parts and torched before dawn) and made Leonard Curtis's corpse fill his pockets with rocks and slip into the vile dark waters of the river. Rudy quickly disengaged so he wouldn't feel the suffocating river close over him.

14

Over the next year, Rudy regrouped.

He reported his mother's car as stolen and retooled his microchip designs to find the flaw that had allowed the last woman to fight back so viciously. Meanwhile, the killings stopped. The city relaxed.

When all was ready, Rudy started up again. He put another ad in the back of the *Village Voice* and online and repeated the process that had led him to his first Special Friend.

His *first*… sitting in a dark corner of a deli on 86th Street in Manhattan on another Halloween, watching one of his new possibilities fidget with his watch as he waited for the date that would never show up, Rudy realized the truth of that word: *first*. Leonard Curtis could really be only the beginning of an endless line of Special Friends who would long serve his purposes.

And then, he thought, following the man out of the coffee shop and into the penumbra of the night (he had already decided this one wouldn't do; not handsome enough in real life), stepping around the little bastards in their costumes begging for treats, once he had sufficiently intimidated New York City, he could move on to somewhere else. The world was filled with women who needed to be taught a lesson. And pliant men whom he could bend to his will as simple automatons. In fact, he could raise an entire army of them, a battalion he could move as he wished… there would be no end to it.

Thus distracted by his thoughts, he wasn't aware of the figure waiting in the dark corner of the garage. Not until he let himself into his apartment and felt himself grabbed from behind with the barrel of a gun against his temple.

He raised his hands. His heart quickened; when all was said and done, Rudy was a coward. "I don't have any money. It's all just junk here, as you can see."

The figure behind him sighed. "Oh, Rudy, Rudy, Rudy…"

Wait—was that a woman's voice?

It sounded like—could it be?

It was unmistakable.

Rudy spun around. "You!"

"Surprised?"

"What are you doing here?! I told you never to come down here!"

Rudy Peppers's mother took a step back, keeping the gun trained on him. "I've been down here lots of times," said Mabel Peppers. "I know all your dirty little secrets, my son, my son. I know just what you've been up to in this hell hole."

She waved the gun, indicating the electronics on the door he used as a desk. "Interesting setup," she said. "That microchip over there, is that what you've been working on?"

"How would you know about that?"

"Please. You know your trouble? You always think you're smarter than everybody else. I was poking around down here one day—yes, yes, I come down quite a bit while you're at work—and I was playing with your little toys, pushing buttons to see what would happen, and after a while I heard a banging on the garage door. Turns out I accidently summoned your monster."

"He's not a monster. He's my Special Friend. But yes, that's the next generation microchip," Rudy said proudly. "I just haven't had a chance to… to try it out yet."

"You mean you haven't found your latest killer?"

"How can you possibly know about all this?"

"If you'd ever showed the slightest interest in me or your late father, you'd know we met at the Bell Labs in New Jersey where we were both engineers. Except I gave up my career to raise a family. Unfortunately, the only child we were able to have… was you. So you came by your technological expertise through us."

She sighed again. "But Rudy… *why* would you kill all those innocent women?"

"They weren't innocent," he snarled. "They deserved to die for what they did to me."

"They didn't even know you."

"It doesn't matter. I sacrificed them in the name of all the others."

"What others?"

"You wouldn't understand."

"You got that right, you little freak," Mabel muttered. She placed the microchip on the desk top and with the butt of her gun crushed the tiny wafer.

"You think that'll stop me?" he sneered. "There'll be a hundred more where that came from. A thousand!"

She shook her head. "If you weren't such a monster, you'd be pathetic."

"There's going to be a whole army at my command!"

"No, son," she said. "Your days as a destroyer are over."

"They've only just begun, you stupid fucking cow!"

"Tell me, though," she said, "did you ever find out what went wrong with your last one? Wasn't he supposed to kill that Taylor woman just like the others?"

"She's dead."

"But not like the others. No strangulation, no clown makeup… And where is your souvenir of the kill?"

"It was problems with the circuitry in the chip," he said, ignoring her question. "But don't worry. I fixed it. And I'm ready to start again."

She pulled a ham radio handset out of her housecoat and turned it on. "I have some bad news for you, my son. There wasn't anything wrong with the chip itself. It was the neurotransmitter. That's where your problem was."

He watched her through narrowed eyes. "How do you know?"

She punched in numbers on the handset with her forefinger. "After I realized you were behind the killings, I came in here and checked out your work."

"How did you know it was me?"

"I read about the killings in the newspaper. On one of my visits down here I found your box of trophies. Everything was there, from the first waitress's ID badge—poor Fiona—to the real estate agent's broach. I realized you were the Ghoul."

She shook her head again. "Shouldn't have kept souvenirs, you silly, flawed boy."

Rudy heard a crash against the garage doors beside his apartment. "What's that?"

"Flawed," she repeated, ignoring his question, "and monstrous. Such a disappointment."

Another crash, this time like a body lurching against the garage door.

"All you needed to transmit successfully," she said, "without any foul-ups, is in this little critter right here." She held up her handset. "Nothing wrong with the microchip at all."

She punched in more numbers and something banged against the garage door again, harder this time.

A great fear gripped Rudy's heart.

"What is that? What are you going to do to me?" he cried.

"Relax, my boy," Mabel said. "I'm not going to hurt you."

She crossed the room and threw open the door leading to the garage. "But *he* will."

Standing in the doorway, dripping wet, body skeletal, his fine wardrobe now hanging from his bones in sopping rags, one arm gone, face mostly gone and what was left the color of a fish's belly, the microchip visible and lodged in the side of his head, was what remained of Leonard Curtis after having reposed at the bottom of the East River.

Rudy could only stare in horror.

Mabel entered more numbers on her handset and Leonard's bony corpse shuffled into the room, leaving a trail of rank river water. One foot was missing and all the finger bones were gone from his one hand. His foul stench made Rudy's eyes water.

"He's a little the worse for wear," she admitted. "Still works pretty well, though. You shouldn't have left the microchip embedded in his skull."

"What — how — ?"

She punched a code into her handset and the ruins of Leonard Curtis shuffled closer.

"Gah!" Rudy said.

"Afraid?" his mother asked.

He nodded mutely.

"Good. Now you know how those poor women felt. I hate to do this to you, Rudy, especially since I'm only — how did you just put it? A 'stupid fucking cow'? But I have to make sure you never harm another woman, ever again."

"Get him away from me! I swear I'll never do it again!"

"Sorry, Rudy. No more lies. And no more killing."

Leonard's filthy ruins edged closer, driving Rudy back against his desk.

"The funny thing is," his mother said, "even after all this time in the water he still seems to remember those lessons you taught him. About how to hurt people, I mean."

"You're not really going to do this, are you, Mother? Momma? Mommy!"

She gave the number pad of her handset a light tap and Leonard leaned forward and felled Rudy with one blow from his remaining arm like a soggy tree limb.

"No," Rudy cried, "this can't be happening!"

"Oh, I'm afraid it very much is."

Even minus his fingers, what was left of Leonard was still powerful enough to crush the life out of Rudy Peppers in very little time.

The last things Rudy saw before his final darkness set in were the lower halves of the neighborhood children's Halloween costumes passing his window—blue leggings and red boots of Spiderman outfits, teal gowns of Princess Elsas, yellow capes and goggles of Minions, and many other costumes that he would never be able to identify any more.

DREAD BOX

Andrew Charles Lark

I see you're courting more despair.
No hope? Not a glimmer.
> —Brian Ferry, "Casanova"

1

Halloween, 2020

"Darling, I think they're closed," said Grandma.

"Bullshit!" replied Grampa, pulling into the parking lot of the fifth, incredibly boring antique shop of the day. "It's ten 'til and they're not closed until after we leave. That's how it works." Grampa maneuvered his ancient, black, mint-condition Cadillac Fleetwood Brougham into the closest spot, then shut the behemoth down with a twist of the key. David sat behind Grampa in the back seat, smothered in plush, cushioned, mahogany leather in a resigned state of despair. They had promised that they would drop him off at his friend Zach's to go trick-or-treating, then he was going to spend the night.

It was Saturday, literally the best day for Halloween. It had been a beautiful, sunny, late October day, with a promised evening of warm weather that couldn't have been more perfect. David's costume was packed into his overnight bag that lay on the wool carpet on the rear passenger side footwell, behind Grandma. "Bags on the floor—not the seat!" barked Grampa when they'd set off six hours earlier, "It'll scuff the leather."

"Grampa, would you mind if Grandma dropped me off at my friend Zach's while you're in there?" asked David. "I was going to trick-or-treat, then spend the night, remember?"

"Jesus Christ almighty! How old are you again?"

"I'm thirteen," replied David through gritted teeth. Grandma turned toward David and gave him a quick wink as she unbuckled, then turned back and flipped the visor down.

"Thirteen? Really? I thought you were twelve! When did you turn thirteen?" Grandma peered into the vanity mirror to check the sun visor that had been artfully incorporated into her poofy hairdo.

"Last week," said David.

"Oh!" replied Grandma. Her eyes betrayed a perplexed and slightly embarrassed crinkle that David caught in the reflection from his vantage in the back. "Well... happy birthday," she said, flipping the visor back up, "and I don't drive, sweetie. I used to have a driver, but Grampa fired him after he retired. Now Grampa's my driver," she said, patting Grampa's shoulder, her face set in an artificial smile to counter the dark mood that permeated the gaudy interior of the old, 1970s Cadillac. Grampa's shoulder recoiled from her touch.

"Thirteen and he wants to go trick-or-treating," said Grampa, fingering a wad of bills in his cash belt. "They coddled him, can you see that now?"

"Well, he misses his friends. Do you miss your friends, Davie?" said Grandma.

"It's David. And yes, I miss my friends."

"Don't correct your grandmother!"

"Gordon, Please! Go easy. Davie's been through a lot this year, haven't you, Davie?" said Grandma. She donned her giant, round sunglasses, the ones with the white frames and green lenses. Just then David's cellphone buzzed. He fished it from his pocket and read the text from Zach:

"WTF!!! 5 and we bail!!! Hry up!!!"

"Would you mind if I waited in the car," asked David. "Apparently I gotta let my friends know that I'm not coming now."

"Oh, we're sorry sweetie."

"I'm not," said Grampa. "When I was thirteen I already had ten grand in the bank, and all junior back there wants to do is go door to door begging for handouts!"

"I mean, my friends are waiting for me, and I gotta let them know that I'm not coming," said David, holding his cellphone up so Grampa could see that he was serious, and not just making excuses. Besides, he never wanted to step foot inside another dusty, smelly, nasty, musty, antique shop as long as he lived.

"I don't see why he can't wait in the car," said Grandma. "Sure, you can—"

"NO! He's coming in with us." Grampa leaned into Grandma's ear and half-whispered, "This is an old car. What if he figures out how to hotwire it with that cockamamie cellphone thing of his."

"I literally don't know what you're talking about," said David, his ire increasing by the second. Grampa had been an insufferable prick from the minute David walked through their door seven months prior, juggling a giant suitcase and three boxes. Grampa didn't even bother to help. He simply beelined into the library to pour himself another high-ball, probably.

"Alright... hand it over," said Grampa.

"What?" said David.

"I want that cellphone. C'mon... give it up," said Grampa, his open palm hovering over the front seat arm rests. "If I know you, you're plotting away on that thing, and I'm tired of hearing it buzz every five seconds."

"You can't be serious," said David, his anger now super-charged with panic. "How am I supposed to talk to my friends?"

"Maybe it's time you made new friends," said Grampa. "You know... in your new school?"

"Gordon. Let him be, please."

"Goddammit Phyllis, NO! We'll come out and the car will be gone! I'm not risking it, and that's final. Now we've wasted enough time. Everybody out!"

2

March 13, 2020

David was sitting in third hour when the school counselor, Mrs. Lewis, came to the classroom door and gestured through the window for Mrs. Fallow, David's English teacher, to come out to the hall. David watched them talk. Mrs. Fallow's shoulders slumped and her eyes welled with tears, then her lips formed the words, *"Oh no!"* A minute later she called David out to the hallway. Mrs. Lewis walked David down to her office, sat him down and told him that his grandparents would be arriving shortly to pick him up. David noticed that a box of Kleenex had been pre-placed on the table close to where she'd asked him to sit.

"Why? What's going on? Tell me," asked David, a knot forming in his stomach.

"David, I have terrible news, and there's no easy way to tell you this," said Mrs. Lewis. Her voice cracked. "Two hours ago, your mother and father were killed in a car accident. I know that this is shocking, and I'm so sorry. I'm so very, very sorry for you."

Everything after that was a blur: Mrs. Lewis taking him to his locker and David trying the combination three times before getting it right, snatching glimpses of his peers as he walked by classroom doors and every single one of them oblivious to his shock. He stopped when he saw his best friend Zach, and when they made eye contact, Zach's face read like a question mark, but then he gave David a *call me* gesture. David nodded. They walked into the office and the school secretary glanced nervously at David, then quickly left her chair and disappeared down the admin hall. Zach texted David:

"Bro, whut up? You busted?"

"No. Talk later."

"Cmon... tell me!!!"

"Srsly bro... I can't even right now. TTYL."

"Yer skarin me!"

David shut his phone down and stuffed it into his jacket pocket. He sat in the office with his book bag packed full, waiting and waiting, and watching the clock, and waiting for over two hours for his grandparents to arrive... the grandparents he'd seen precisely twice in his life even though they lived only twenty miles away.

3

Halloween, 2020

This antique shop looked just like all the others with its crappy, dusty light fixtures hanging from the ceiling, pegboard dividers separating vignettes of more crap, curios filled with Hummel figurines, Roseville pottery, Blenko glassware, Libby, Georges Briard shit, naked lady ashtrays, mid-century modern this and art deco that... and the only reason that David knew what he was looking at was because Grandma had been kind enough on previous antique excursions to point at things and give him little lessons in crap:

"Now this is Roseville, and here's how you can tell... and this is a Hummel figurine. I think they're adorable, don't you? I have a curio filled with them in the drawing room. I'll show you when we get home." At least Grandma was nice, but Grampa would say without fail as he pushed through the door of any given antique shop, "Put your hands in your pockets, and don't touch anything. I'll be goddamned if I'm buying anything that you break!"

Such a fucking prick, thought David, watching his fat-ass in those baggy khakis beeline ahead to inspect, complain, and haggle. David noticed that more than a few of the proprietors would roll their eyes when Grampa walked in. They remembered this old fuck from the last time he'd darkened their day with his bullshit. *Gimme a break, you old fuck... and you can start by dropping dead!* said their exasperated eyes.

David had to admit that this shop was not without a few cool things. There was this big, old music box that played old-timey music by means of a spinning metal disc with rectangular holes punched into it. David walked up to three beautifully carved and colorful carousel horses that were taken from an actual merry-go-round. Their nostrils flared, and their eyes, fierce and determined, but David felt sorry for them because here they just looked sad and trapped. David could identify. Grandma walked up behind David and tapped his shoulder.

"Davie, I know it doesn't seem like it, but your grampa does love you. He's just a gruff, old fuss-budget sometimes."

"More like all the time," said David.

"I understand how you feel, but he's just set in his ways. Give him some time to get used to things, okay? Oh, those poor horses. I hope they find a nice home soon," said Grandma.

"I was just thinking the same thing," said David.

"I'm sorry that we forgot your birthday last week, so Grampa wants you to pick something out, okay? Nothing too expensive though," said Grandma with a wink.

"I dunno," said David.

"Please?" said Grandma. "Maybe it'll help break the ice between you two."

David thought about it for a second. "Alright. I'll look around."

"You do that, sweetie. In case you haven't noticed, I love to shop."

"Oh, I've noticed," said David, smiling for the first time all day.

"I can help if you like," offered Grandma.

"Okay," said David, "you go this way, and I'll go that way."

"Atta boy!" she said, ruffling his hair. They turned and went in opposite directions.

The old wood floor creaked underfoot as David walked toward the back of the shop. Up ahead loomed a doorway with glass beads hanging from the header. Crucifixes, Stars of David, the Eye of Horus, an Ankh, and small strands of dried sage looped into crosses were nailed around its opening. A bowl of holy water rested on a podium just to the left, and if David read Latin he would have understood that the phrase scrawled above the doorway in lamb's blood,

Spem Derelinquentes Omnes Qui Intratis

meant Abandon All Hope Ye Who Enter. David parted the beads and walked through.

The light was different in this backroom annex — off-kilter, where shadows had the advantage. A darkness lurked off to David's left where a figure stood atop a box dressed in an old, tea-stained wedding gown. *Creepy mannequins... great,* thought David as he walked by, not even wanting to look at it... but had David looked he would have seen a face so etched in hatred that the air around it literally vibrated. He would have noticed milky eyes that followed him as he walked through the annex jammed with artifacts from the Victorian era: an old rocking horse with a tattered cushioned seat, a crystal chandelier that couldn't sparkle for all the grime, gaudy furniture upholstered in threadbare silks and satins, their floral and zig-zag patterns cloying and disorienting. If David hadn't turned to inspect a shelf with a trio of small, bronze monkey figurines that heard, saw, nor spoke no evil, he would have seen the figure in the tea-stained wedding gown vanish into the dowry chest on which it stood.

David heard a thump and a metallic click, like a key turning in a lock. Startled, he turned and there in the corner, an ornate box... *or, what did Grandma refer to them as during one of her crap lessons? A hope chest? A dowry box?*

Like the other objects in this room, it was very ornate, but more Art Nouveau than Victorian. It was decorated with scores of long, sinewy, gold vines inlaid into the ebony wood. The vines curved and twisted elegantly around the corners and spilled over onto the top, each vine terminating in ivory inlaid lily blooms sprouting from their tips. On the front of the box was a weird woman in a long gown holding a silver tray with a man's head on it. Blood dripped from the tray onto her feet.

Very creepy. Very cool, thought David. *I bet this thing's way too expensive for Grampa, though.* David approached the box and looked for a price tag but found none. It was cold in this corner; a chill tingled up his neck and down his arms, raising goose bumps, and his breath steamed when he exhaled. *Damn,* he thought. *Turn the heat up back here!* He blew into his palms, crouched, then tried opening the lid, but it was locked, or maybe it was jammed shut. Too hard to tell in the murk. David had forgotten all about what he thought was a mannequin in the tea-stained wedding gown.

"It was here before I opened, and that was twenty-nine years ago," said Mr. Hintermann, the proprietor of the antique shop. His fingers trembled as he ran them through his comb-over. "I remember speaking to the woman I bought this place from, and she'd told me it had been here back when she opened too, and that was in, what... '51? So I honestly don't think there's a person alive who knows how long that dowry chest has been sitting here."

David thought it was odd that Mr. Hintermann stood in the doorway and wouldn't walk into the room. *And why does he look so nervous,* he wondered. He was thin and slight with bad posture, and seemed weighed down by the thick, brown, craftsman's leather apron he wore.

"Alright, let's get down to brass tacks," said Grampa. "It's got a crack on the left side under the handle, the bottom's dry-rotted, and I doubt very much that it's ebony." He was in full-on haggle mode, and it was actually kind of fun watching him bullshit his way toward a price he was willing to pay.

"Oh, it's ebony," said Mr. Hintermann. He pulled a small notebook and pen from his apron pocket and began to scribble. "And I'll put that in writing for you."

David stepped away from the negotiation and walked down a narrow aisle brimming with dark things. He looked up through the filthy industrial window and even though the sunny day had reached gloaming, the light that filtered through was gray and dank. Bored, he turned and joined Grandma who stood next to a tall, narrow birdcage. He had to get his cellphone back from the old prick. He had to know what was going on, but mostly he had to tell Zach how his grandfather reneged on everything, and why he couldn't go trick-or-treating tonight. Yes, the box was cool, but in no way did it make up for what a colossal prick he was being.

"And the metal inlay is probably brass," countered Grampa.

"No, it's gold. I'll put that in writing too," parried Mr. Hintermann.

"Okay, so it's got all the bells and whistles. What're you asking?" Grampa took his cash belt out.

"What are you offering?"

"Well, it's got those condition issues... hold-up. Give me five minutes. I want to look it over a little more carefully."

"Sure thing," said Mr. Hintermann. "I'll be back in five." He turned and left. David heard the soft pace of his footfalls slowly recede down the creaky wood floor toward the front of the shop.

Grampa turned to Grandma and for the first time since he'd moved in with them, David saw Grampa smile, but truth be told, it was actually more of a shit-eating grin.

"Alright listen," said Grampa, "this is crazy, but I don't think that clown knows what he's got here. This dowry box is definitely French, probably 1890s, and made from the highest quality materials—ebony, gold, and the locking mechanism is Louis Vuitton, as is all the brightwork, so it's probably a custom, one-of-a-kind. The inlay is exquisite, and if I'm not mistaken, that's a genuine Aubrey Beardsley illustration that's been filigreed in gold and silver on the face."

Grandma knew a thing or two about antiques too, and had a great eye for details. She crouched and pulled a jeweler's loupe from her handbag and studied the inlay.

"It's not silver. It's platinum," said Grandma. "Silver tarnishes."

"Okay, platinum. Even better. Regardless, this dowry box is a masterpiece... a world-class national treasure of the highest order. This thing's worth north of five grand, and on a good day, more like six. Okay, kid," said Grampa. "This box is coming home with us. Watch and learn." David turned from the penny-farthing he was looking at and gave Grampa an unsure smile.

A minute later Mr. Hintermann parted the beads and stood in the doorway. By now Grampa had walked deeper into the room and scrutinized a tri-panel Chinese room divider, and Grandma was busy inspecting a bowl that looked to be jade, but she had her doubts. Mr. Hintermann cleared his throat.

"Folks, have you given any more thought to the dowry box? By no means do I want to rush you, but I did close forty minutes ago." Grampa walked a little further up the aisle then turned.

"What? Oh yeah, the box," said Grampa, pretending to have forgotten about it. "I noticed some pretty serious condition issues under the left handle, and the bottom is dry-rotted. You know, it's gonna cost me a pretty penny to have it restored properly, and I don't know if I want to go to all that trouble."

"Make me an offer," said Mr. Hintermann. "I'll work with you, here."

"Okay, I'll give you one-hundred-bucks... out the door."

"HA! Twenty-five is my..."

"Twenty-five-hundred? Forget about it. You're not getting anything close to that with those condition issues."

"Not twenty-five-hundred. Twenty-five... as in dollars."

"Okay, now you're insulting my intelligence. Twenty-five-dollars, huh? Alright, let's cut the shit here. You and I both know this box is worth at least a hundred, so what's the deal? Why are you giving it away?"

"What's the deal? I'll tell you the deal, and folks, please excuse my language," said Mr. Hintermann, glancing at Grandma and David, "but I just want this abomination the hell out of my shop. I'll write up a bill of sale and it's yours. That's it, plain and simple." Grampa cocked his head and his eyes went to saucers, like a gambler pulling in a giant pile of chips after setting his royal flush onto the green felt.

"What do you mean by abomination?" asked Grandma. "Wait a minute!" her eyes lit up. "Are you saying this piece is haunted?"

"That's exactly what I'm saying," said Mr. Hintermann.

"Oh, then we've got to have it!" said Grandma. "That stuff is so fascinating! I have a medium friend I'd love to have over, and... "

"Oh come on!" interrupted Grampa. "I don't believe any of that haunted furniture B.S., and there have been plenty of articles about that malarky in some of the trade magazines. Now, because I have scruples, here's my original offer of one-hundred dollars. Don't insult me with your ridiculous twenty-five-dollar counter-offer. For that extra seventy-five you can help the kid load it into my car."

"Gladly," said Mr. Hintermann, taking Grampa's hundred-dollar bill. "Pleasure doing business with you."

A bill of sale was handed over and the antique dowry box was loaded into the cavernous trunk of the Fleetwood. They drove the thirty miles back toward the Pointes, where Jefferson turned into Lake Shore. Grampa turned left on Bishop, drove up a couple of blocks, turned right, and a sensor buried deep in the Caddy's guts activated the gate which opened onto a vast lawn, dotted with clusters of towering elms, tastefully understated landscaping, and a large pond off to the right. The long blacktop driveway curved, and around the bend lay a massive, Tudor mansion... twenty-five-thousand square feet of ostentatious opulence due mostly to Grandma's over-the-top taste that leaned wholly toward Hollywood Regency.

It was now well past 10:00 p.m. and the trick-or-treaters had long since abandoned the streets and made their way back to their homes.... but it wasn't like Bishop got many trick-or-treaters anyway because the massive properties here were measured, not in square feet but in acres, making Bishop Street a Halloween dead-zone. No-one walked Bishop. It was a street comprised solely of wealthy, entitled, connected, old-money titans ensconced in their estates, and excepting the old money, Grampa fit right in.

Yeah, I found that box fair and square, but the old fuck keeps going on and on about it like it's the antique score of the century, thought David. *And it probably is thanks to me. Oh well, who cares. He'll probably renege on it being my birthday gift, and auction it off just like he does with so much of his other antique crap. But that's not gonna happen. It's my box, and I'll die before he gets his greedy paws on it.*

The dowry box was heavy and schlepping it upstairs to David's third story bedroom—the smallest of the bedrooms and the one furthest down the hall—would have to wait until morning when a crew of workers was scheduled to arrive for various winterization tasks, and hauling a heavy box up three flights of stairs would be added to the list of things to do.

4

November 2, 2020

Since moving into his Grandparent's place, David had been forced to switch from Bromley Middle School to Townsend, in the rich kids' district. The adjustments continued to be tough with virtually everyone letting him know that his place in the pecking order was rock-bottom. Townsend and Bromley were arch-rivals, and this put David in the impossible position of being an enemy invader at Townsend, and a traitor at Bromley.

The bell rang after first hour and eight-hundred kids streamed into the hallways toward their lockers. David had finished twisting out his combination when Dominick and Brent arrived.

"Hey Brent, didja hear about that kid at Bromley?" said Dominick, a few lockers from David's. Dominick was the tallest kid in school but too uncoordinated for sports. His painful shin splints saw to that, and any questions about his game on the basketball court were answered with a pimply sneer.

"No. I don't follow all the goings on at Bromley. Tell me," said Brent, whose locker was next to David's. Brent was one particularly charming motherfucker. He was captain of the lacrosse team and had been assigned as David's Townsend Student Ambassador; his duties included introductions, activities, sports, and clubs. He'd come off as super-friendly while the teachers were around, but when no one was looking, he'd smack David into next week and say things like, "You'll never fit in here, trash. Go back to Bromley where you belong."

"Some kid there was hit by a car and killed on Halloween. Such a fuckin' tragedy," said Dominick, rolling his eyes.

"Hmm... thoughts 'n prayers 'n all that jazz." Brent turned and slammed David's locker door shut.

"Did you hear that, shithead? One of your Bromley bros bit it. Tragic, huh? Gee, I hope it wasn't one of your special ed friends. That would be... so... sad," said Brent.

"Thanks for telling me, Brently the Third," said David. Brent hated being call Brently the Third. David re-opened his locker and jammed his foot into the door to prevent further shenanigans.

"Always a pleasure... and Brent will do just fine."

"Asshole works too. And your thoughts 'n prayers 'n all that jazz are most appreciated, Brently the Third." Even though David ranked far below Brent, he still had his pride, and he wasn't in the mood for anyone's shit this morning, mostly because Grampa still hadn't given David his cellphone back and it had become a literal and unbearable form of torture, not knowing what was going on. David had been pretty popular at Bromley, and the chances of him knowing who'd been killed were very high, but the odds of it being a close friend were fairly low, given that there were over seven-hundred kids at Bromley.

Still, he had to know, and thanks to fucking Grampa, he'd been completely cut-off from any and all news. *This is just so fucked. I've got to get my cellphone,* thought David. *Maybe Grandma can talk him into giving it back.*

"Call me Brently the Third one more time and you're going down," said Brent. He tried slamming David's locker shut again, but this time David slid his foot out, grabbed Brent's wrist, held it, and slammed the door on Brent's fingers. Brent howled in pain, clutching his injured hand.

"You fuckin' psycho! You broke my fingers! You're dead, you Bromley piece of shit!"

"Go fuck yourself, Brently the Third," said David, grabbing his books. He slammed his locker door shut and headed off to second hour.

Twenty minutes later David was summoned to the office for an inquiry over an act of violence between classes.

Dr. Whittingham, Townsend's principal, had called David's grandparents to let them know that David was being suspended for five days for an act of violence against a fellow student. He also let them know that in no uncertain terms would Townsend Middle School tolerate any violent, anti-social behavior from its students, and that David would be required to write an essay on why his behavior was wrong, including what steps he would take to manage his anger. He would also be required to meet with the school's counselor twice a week for the rest of the school year.

For this David was sent to his room after dinner, which was actually fine with him. He'd rather be alone in his room with his box anyway.

Grandma had told him that the figure on the front was a very famous Art Nouveau rendering of an Aubrey Beardsley illustration of Salome — a woman who asked for the head of John the Baptist after dancing her dance of the seven veils.

David laid in bed on his side and stared at the box. He admired the sinewy, gold vines that swooped and curved upward and onto the lid, but now they slowly undulated and crept, twisting and growing from off the box toward his bed. And now the vines touched and probed. They played and tugged at him, tested the weight of him, and coiled around and lifted him, cradling him, and oh, how the intoxicating scent of lilies permeated the air. David gazed at the woman holding the platter with the head on it, and wished more than anything that it was Grampa's head laying on the platter, and that it was his blood pouring down onto her shoes. As he stared at the woman, David heard a far-off tinkling of bells, and a strange, exotic music.

The woman turned her gaze upon David as he lay cradled in the golden vines that held him aloft in a lily-scented fever dream. The woman swayed seductively to the ring of the tinkling bells which David felt through the vines, like a spider sensing ensnared prey.

My sweet boy. My sweet, sweet, darling boy. Come to me, love me, and reveal to me all the black things that lurk in your beating heart and release them unto me. Love me and feed me those dark thoughts that afflict your poor, tortured soul, and they will trouble you no more, my sweet prince, my dearest, darling boy. And know this: I am yours... and you are mine, always and forever.

"Yesssss," whispered David, coiled in the ecstasy of these golden vines which continued to undulate above, where lilies popped open and dusted him in their fragrant, toxic pollen.

David had no way of knowing that it was the bride, the woman in the tea-stained wedding gown that he'd caught a glimpse of in his peripheral vision when he first walked into the back annex of the antique shop. She would use David's growing obsession with the box to seduce and to trick. She needed his soul... and she would have it.

5

March 28, 2020

"I'd been casing their place for months and gotten their patterns down to a T but even the best laid plans have their hiccups. You and I both know that." Donny took a long drag off his cigarette and exhaled out the open window. Blue-tinged smoke hovered five feet above the concrete floor in the dim of the ten-car garage.

It was 1 a.m. and they sat in an old, mint condition Mark IV, Donny in the driver's seat and Gordon sitting shotgun. Nine other classic cars from the '50s, '60s, and '70s stood sentry, lined up like soldiers, their gleaming chrome grills facing forward, and every one of them, primo, USDA-certified examples of Detroit Steel. Gordon had an intense passion for two things: classic cars and quality antiques.

"Yeah, well this was one colossal, fucking hiccup. The plan was that the boy's father dies, and NOT his mother. Her dying was NOT part of the plan, and now I got a fuckin' teenager living under my roof."

"What more can I tell you?" said Donny, his gravelly voice rising an octave. "Every morning at 7:45 he pulls out of the garage and drives to work... in his car. Ten minutes later the kid leaves and walks to the corner bus stop. The bus arrives at 8:05 and the kid, along with seven others hop onto the bus and it leaves. Then at 8:30 she pulls out of the garage... in her car, and leaves for work. I could have set my watch to this sequence of events, but on the 13th what happens? He pulls out of the garage at 7:45, once again... in his car. But this time they're both in the car with him. So I follow, but I maintain a certain distance, you know? They drop the kid off at school then head north. Thirty miles later he loses control due to no brakes, swerves, and the car plows into a tree. They're killed instantly."

"Yep. Good job. All except for the fact that now I've got a fucking teenager living under my roof. That was definitely NOT part of the plan," said Gordon.

"None of my business, Gordo. But I still can't figure out why you wanted your own son dead. I had my doubts about this one, I really did."

"HE WASN'T MY KID! HE WAS TWINKLE-TOES TOMMY'S KID! HE HAD TO GO!"

"Alright, alright! Calm down. You're gonna give yourself an embolism," said Donny. He tapped the long ash off his cigarette out the window, adding to the pile of ashes outside the car. Then Donny thought of something else. He looked at Gordon.

"And you know, the 13th was a Friday, and I shoulda known better."

"Don't give me that Friday the 13th crap! That's got nothing to do with nothing."

"Well, at least the investigation went our way," said Donny. "My brake jobs are always undetectable."

"I'll grant you that," said Gordon. "You know your cars and there's no doubt about it. But what the fuck am I supposed to do with a teenager hanging around for the next five years?"

"Don't ask me! Boarding school? It's not my problem and it stays that way! I draw the line at kids... I ain't no kid killer."

"I'm not asking you to take care of the kid. I've got it handled."

"And I don't think I have to remind you about the other problems I've solved for you, do I? Good 'ole Twinkle-toes Tommy, and Toledo Dee?"

"What are you driving at?" said Gordon.

"I'm retiring, and I'm here to collect my pension."

"What the fuck you talking about?"

"I'm out! I'm done driving your wife around, and I'm finished taking care of your problems."

"Fuck! I knew this day would come sooner or later," said Gordon. He lowered his window and futilely waved at smoke. "And gimme a break on the cigarettes, will you? What is that, your fifth? Jesus Christ, you're stinkin' up 'ole Betsy here."

"Well, in addition to the four-million-dollar pension I've got coming, I've been thinking that you'll be throwing in 'ole Betsy here as a bonus... you know, for all my years of dedicated loyalty."

"Four million, huh?"

"Yeah. A million per problem solved. I think that's fair. And let's face it, 'ole Betsy here loves me more than she loves you."

"Izzat so?"

"Absolutely. She purrs like a kitten every time I turn her key. And Gordo, another thing: I'm gettin' too old for this shit. I'm seventy-two fuckin' years old and I'm tired. I'm fuckin' tired Gordo, and I need some tropical beach time before I drop. You know what I'm saying?

"Tropical beach time, huh? And four million is gonna take me a few weeks. We don't want to be raising any eyebrows come tax time. I'll have tracks to cover."

"You got one month."

"Goddammit Donny! You're killin' me."

"Funny... as I recall, Twinkle-toes Tommy and Toledo Dee said words very similar many years ago," said Donny. He whipped out his Zippo, snapped it open, and fired-up another cancer stick.

"You got a month," said Donny, exhaling smoke. "Now I'm taking 'ole Betsy, here. On April 27th, she'll be on the third level of the parking structure on South Lafayette in Royal Oak. On April 28th my pension will be placed into her trunk, and you'll never see nor hear from me again. Got it?"

"Look at Donny with his big, brass balls, sittin' in the driver's seat, callin' all the shots!" said Gordon. His fists were clenched so tightly they could've cracked walnuts.

"Gordo, I only hope you'll remember what a stand-up, loyal employee I've been these past forty years."

"You're right, Donny. You've been my number one for a long time, and you shouldn't have any doubts about that. I'm just giving you all kinds of shit because it's gonna be rough going on without you. I want you to know that."

6

November 3, 2020

Phyllis snatched a Nero Wolfe paperback from a stack of books on her nightstand and slid the feather out that she used as a bookmark, picking up where she left off... but she wasn't really into it tonight.

The door between her room and Gordon's was cocked half-open and she could hear him milling around in his ensuite bath engaged in his nightly bedtime ritual: faucet on, brushing teeth, gargling, and the faint sounds of a dozen pharmaceuticals being ingested. The light snapped off in his ensuite and she heard him trudge toward his bed and get in. A second later the lamp on his nightstand clicked off and his room went dark. Phyllis stuck the feather back in, put her book aside, and called out to Gordon.

"Hey. Come in here and give me my kiss goodnight."

"I'm in bed already," said Gordon.

"You used to give me kisses every night. What's going on with you? Why are you being such a grump lately?"

"Because there's a teenager living under our roof and I'm not happy about it," said Gordon.

Phyllis heard him shifting petulantly around in his bed. *He's literally tossing and turning,* she thought. *He can be so pathetic sometimes.*

"Our grandson, you mean. Our grandson is living under our roof. He's not just some teenager," replied Phyllis. She heard Gordon climb out of his bed then he appeared in the doorway in his striped pajamas.

"Your grandchild, you mean!" said Gordon pointing at her. He's not my grandchild! I don't have any grandchildren, remember?"

"For God's sake! It's not Davie's fault. He had nothing to do with it. And are you ever going to forgive me? How many times do I have to apologize?

"Every time I look at that kid I see Twinkle-toes Tommy."

"Stop it! And you're not exactly Mr. Innocent! Remember Dee? I sure do!"

Gordon balled up his fist and punched the door so hard it vibrated on its hinges.

"Goddammit, Phyllis! He looks just like him!"

"It's not his fault, and I'm getting sick and tired of you treating him like he's some kind of juvenile delinquent," said Phyllis.

"Well, after what he did to that kid in school, that's exactly what he is! A juvenile delinquent!"

"For God's sake, he lost his parents in a car accident a few months ago, and he's got nobody except us. Would you please try to be nice to him? He's been through a lot, and you know it."

"So have I," said Gordon turning around and stomping back into his room. "And don't get too attached to him, Phyllis. I've been looking around, and after I find the most hard-core military boarding school there is, he's gone, and don't think I'm kidding around. I want Twinkle-toes junior the fuck out of my sight, and that's all there is to it."

Now it was Phyllis who got out of bed. She appeared in the doorway.

"Gordon? Turn around. Look at me." Gordon turned. "If he goes... I go," said Phyllis, her index finger accentuating her threats with points and jabs. "I'll take my millions, and Davie, and we'll live happily ever after, and you can fuck-off with another one of your cheap whores in the back seat of one of your old jalopies. Have I made myself perfectly clear?"

"Phyllis." A voice she hadn't heard in over forty years called from the far-off vestibule. She sat up in bed and pulled her sleeping mask off. She heard Gordon snoring away, the door separating their bedrooms now closed.

"Phyllis, come dance with me."

"Tommy?" she whispered. Her old ballroom dancing partner. Dim light filtered in through the window's sheer curtains, and the gilt clock on the fireplace mantel read 3:05. She slid into her slippers and silk kimono and padded down the long hallway. Something stopped her at the top of the stairs: a brilliant, blue eye glinting in one of the crystals of the massive, Swarovski chandelier that hung elegantly over the three-story vestibule. Tommy's eye!

Tommy had strikingly beautiful blue eyes that sparkled, sapphire-like in the pulsing lights of the dance hall. His waspish waist cut an elegant figure, and his sense of timing was unmatched, as was his footwork, but everything he did, she did backwards. In a word, on the dance floor, they were perfection, and their awards, trophies, and blue ribbons could have filled a dozen curio cabinets.

Another brilliant blue eye glinted in the adjacent crystal, and now she really looked and saw his entire form refracting in the crystals, his left arm behind his back, and his right arm arched elegantly outward, beckoning her onto the dance floor.

"Phyllis." She looked down from the top of the stairway, and standing under the chandelier was Tommy in a tailored tuxedo and patent leather dance shoes, his shiny black hair parted to the side with one disheveled shock pointing toward those baby blues.

"Oh, Tommy," said Phyllis with tears streaming down her cheeks. "I've missed you so much." Tommy looked up at her and Phyllis saw that a great sorrow had clouded his visage, and that he now looked too thin and drawn... he was wasting away before her eyes, his cheeks hollowed and his lips, a disturbing shade of blue. It was cold and Phyllis drew her collar close around her neck.

"He did it, Phyllis. He killed our son."

"Tommy, what are you saying?"

"He killed him... he killed all of us." And down in the dark, under the chandelier Phyllis now saw a gathering of poor souls, their dead faces staring up at her—all of whom died mysteriously: Tommy—her lover and dance partner; Dee—Gordon's mistress; Alex—her son and David's father; and Madeline—her daughter-in-law, and David's mother.

"Who killed him, Tommy?" Tommy just smiled sadly and extended his right arm outward.

Further down the hall behind Phyllis stood a woman in a tea-stained wedding gown. Her hair undulated, defying gravity and the scent of lilies perfumed the air around her. A wrathful, hateful malevolence radiated off the bride. Her vibrations altered the atmosphere, causing doors and passages to open through which dark things emerged from their dark places, bringing forth these poor, dark souls that now stood under the chandelier looking up at Phyllis.

Phyllis looked into Tommy's eyes and now she saw only him. Her partner and lover.

Gordon and Phyllis had been high school sweethearts. She was the unattainable rich girl living in her mansion on Windmill Pointe, and he was the rebellious troublemaker and hustler who lived north of Mack Avenue. He'd gotten himself into a jam and the judge gave him a choice: jail or service. Gordon chose and went off to serve a two-year stint in the Navy, leaving Phyllis in the care of Twinkle-toes Tommy... the dancing boy everyone thought was queer. It was the perfect arrangement; better to have him looking after her than risking her being stolen by some horny asshole while he was away.

It started off innocently enough: a look, a blush, or a touch that was difficult to interpret. The way his finger lingered around the back of her neck that caused a chill, or when during a lift, she'd felt his finger wriggle between her lips which made her so wet and flushed — the shock and excitement. Nothing was said, but it was his eyes that sometimes betrayed his thoughts. Sometimes their rehearsals were so sexually charged that she could barely drive the two miles back to her home, and other times there'd be nothing... just business as usual, and it was the wondering about things that was so frustrating... and so alluring. Then one day after a particularly grueling two-hour session where they'd practiced some new, and very complicated moves, mistakes had been made, an ankle twisted, feelings had been hurt, tensions were high, and tempers flared. She walked over to an old, long wooden table and grabbed her towel from the back of a chair. She noticed him approach from behind in the mirror, then she felt the warmth and humidity radiating off his lithe body. He wrapped his arms tightly around her and buried his face into her sweaty mane.

"I'm sorry," he said. "You're perfection. It's all my fault. Forgive me." He parted her hair from her neck with his fingers and passionately kissed her neck. She took a deep breath and fell into him, accepting his passion. She turned and wrapped her arms around him and threw herself into his kiss. Their bodies glistened with sweat as they kissed. He cupped and caressed her breast with one hand and pressed her ass into his groin with his other hand, and their bodies quivered, incapable of keeping up with their raw desire.

These were the thoughts that replayed in Phyllis's mind as she stared down at her long dead Tommy. The others had receded back into their dark places, but Tommy remained a minute longer, his left arm behind his back, and his right arm, elegantly extended toward her, inviting her for one last dance. He slowly dissipated to nothing under the shadow of the giant chandelier which inexplicably rocked slowly from its chain, its crystals tinkling in the dim.

"Tommy," she whispered. Then something else flashed in one of the crystals that startled Phyllis: a dead, milky, white eye, and a face that radiated dread and hatred. Phyllis turned but saw nothing. She winced at the sickly scent of rotting flowers that putrefied the hallway.

7

November 6, 2020

Out of nowhere, something lit-up on the small nightstand next to David's bed that cast his room in an eerie glow. It startled him awake. *Oh my God! My phone! Finally!* he thought, frantically reaching for it. The time at the upper-left corner of the screen indicated 3:07 a.m. He accessed his messages and literally hundreds and hundreds of texts had completely blown up his cellphone since his grandfather had confiscated it six days prior. He opened the text at the top of the scroll. It was from Zach:

"Why didn't you come to my funeral?"

Puzzled, David's heart skipped a beat, then he chuckled and texted back:

"LOL. Why u up so late?"

"Look up," texted Zach.

David looked. Zach hovered inches above the dowry box glowering hatefully at David. He was cast in the dim of the cellphone's light. There was a deep, vertical gash above his left eye, and his head was crooked, his neck no longer capable of bearing its weight. David jumped involuntarily backward and a scream caught in his throat. His back now resting on the steel frame of his bed, he stared at his dead friend terrified, clutching his blanket at his neck, afraid to move another muscle.

"It was you," whispered David. "What happened?"

Zach wailed out a high-pitched cry.

"I waited for you!" sobbed the dead boy.

David shut his eyes tightly and blocked his ears with his arms, and for the first time since he was five, he pissed his bed. After a minute David opened his eyes but Zach was still there staring at David hatefully, daring him to say something. David gathered enough courage to finally clear his parched throat.

"They wouldn't take me. And he took my phone," said David. "Please believe me." He watched horrified as the gash in Zach's head leaked. David's breath steamed in the cold, and the putrid scent of rotting flowers filled the room. Zach stepped unsteadily from above the box and limped toward David's bed, his right leg dragging, but with every step, his form hazed-over in wisps and trails of smoky ectoplasm.

"I waited for you. It's your fault," echoed Zach's cries as he disappeared back to the dark place from whence he came.

David lay there petrified and shaking for what seemed like hours, but when he finally got the courage to move, he checked his phone. Only seven minutes had lapsed. He scrolled back through the text threads chronologically to Halloween night. Eddy, Mario, Will, and Joel were all at Zach's waiting for David, and their texts had started off friendly enough, but the later it got, the more the texts had become laden with sarcasm and even anger.

Mario: *Looks like the Townsend boy is too good for us Bromley boys. LOL*

Eddy: *Bro! Fukin lame to dis us!!!!*

Will: *Whatever, dude!!!*

And then the texts from Zach. He picked up from the last one he had seen, which was:

Zach: *"WTF!!! 5 and we bail!!! Hry up!!!"*

And the rest he hadn't read yet...

Zach: *Bro! Where u at? I tole the others to go. I'll wait for u, but hry up!!!*

Zach: *Bro!!!??? I can't wait anymore!!! Y u bein so lame!!! Leaving now!!! Hope ur here when we get back at least!!!*

Then the tragic accident.

From what David could gather, Zach had run out of his house in order to catch up with his friends whom he had told to go on without him, but when he ran across the street he was struck by an SUV. The impact was so great that his body was thrown and his head and neck struck a large tree trunk, killing him instantly.

There was a litany of very sad texts from his closest friends, peripheral friends, and even Zach's mother, who wondered why

David hadn't reached out. At first the texts were sad and sympathetic, but as the days wore on, their tone shifted to anger and outrage. They expressed how betrayed they felt, and how he'd completely turned his back on all his friends in their hours of pain and sorrow, and how Zach didn't deserve to be treated with such disrespect by his so-called best friend.

And yesterday, the funeral: Some had held out hope that David would show up at least, but because he knew nothing about what had happened, he was obviously a no-show, and for his closest friends this was the tipping point. David's betrayal was a bridge too far. They were the pall-bearers for Zach's casket, but they had decided that there would be four guys on one side, and three on the other, the blank spot obviously meant to be filled by David... a symbol of his desertion.

He was *persona non grata* at Bromley where he no longer had a single, solitary friend. His alienation was complete. He thought about texting everyone about what had happened, but the idea of groveling and making excuses somehow repulsed him, and the hole in his heart went to pitch-black. He stood on his piss-soaked mattress and hurled his cellphone at the wall as hard as he could. He no longer cared. He stripped off his soiled pajama bottoms, dried himself, and put on a new pair, then he flipped the cheap spring mattress over and jumped into it.

With bitter tears streaming down his face, he reached in the dark toward his box. He needed the vines to entwine and lift him, to comfort and sooth him with their fragrance, their vibrations, bells, and music. Very soon he felt the golden vines lace through and between his fingers, then up his arms, legs, and around his torso. As they tickled he smiled through his tears.

They lifted and held him aloft, rocking him slowly in a golden, silky embrace. Then he heard the bells tinkle, and the exotic music echo, and the woman, his goddess spoke soothingly:

Sleep my prince, and gain your strength. And when they come to accuse and torture you, I will be waiting, and this I promise... they will know my wrath and shall never hurt you again. Now rest, my sweet, darling prince. Lie still in my loving embrace. Trust only in me, and know that I will always protect you from those who seek to destroy you.

"Yesssss," he whispered. David inhaled deeply as motes of pollen rained down, lulling him into a euphoric state of oblivion.

November 7, 2020

David and Grandma sat in the breakfast nook conservatory while a cold, cloudy day blustered on the other side of the glass panes and wrought iron that surrounded them. Potted plants, vines, and greenery grew with abandon in the ornate space, and water burbled in a small fountain a few feet away. A pane of glass that needed repointing rattled above in the stronger gusts. This informal breakfast twosome had become a morning ritual over the last month, Grandma with her daily cup of decaf and English muffin, and David with his jelly toast and orange juice.

Phyllis had just finished doing her stretching and exercises in her studio. For a woman in her late 70s, she was in phenomenal shape. She was in her warm-up gear with a hand towel still around her neck.

"I'm sorry that I look so disheveled, Davie, but I just finished my exercises, and now I need my coffee, muffin, and breakfast with my smart grandson," she said with a smile on her face, pouring coffee into her cup. David shyly returned her smile.

"And one more thing, Davie, I don't want to harp, but did you finish that writing assignment for Dr. Whittingham?"

"I'm almost finished with it," said David.

"I know you're a good boy, and you've been through so much, but make sure you finish it, okay?"

"I will. I promise."

They sat in silence as the blustery day raged outside. The loose pane rattled in its frame above Phyllis.

"Grandma, I have to ask, did you bring me my cellphone while I was sleeping last night?"

"Your cellphone? No, it wasn't me. You got it back?"

"Yes. But if it wasn't you, then it must've been Grampa."

"Well, it wasn't me, so it must've been him, but..." Phyllis looked up at the pane that rattled, with her face belying a slightly troubled look. "I told your Grampa a year ago that that pane needs to be fixed, but he still hasn't gotten around to it."

"But what," said David. He had gotten used to how she would trail off and stray from the conversation, especially when discussing things that made her uncomfortable.

"What, but what, sweetie?" replied Grandma.

"You were going to say something about Grampa and my phone."

"Oh! Well, that would be so out of character for him. He hates cellphones. I don't know if you've noticed, but neither of us has one."

"I did notice that," replied David. Grandma trailed off again with a far-off look in her eye. She took a sip of decaf and placed her cup back onto the saucer.

"Davie, would you mind if I allowed a friend up into your room to take a look at your box?"

David's mood suddenly shifted. He was sure that his worst fear was being realized and that they were going to sell his box after all for a big profit because they'd gotten it so cheap.

"For what? To appraise it? You're gonna sell it, aren't you!" said David, accusing more than asking. He jumped up and the chair he was sitting on fell over behind him. "You can't do that! That's my box!"

"Sweetie, no! Of course not! And I don't appreciate the loud accusations," said Grandma.

"I'm sorry. It's just... knowing Grampa, I wouldn't be surprised."

"Davie, I prefer a civilized breakfast, and I don't like being shouted at. Do you understand?"

"Yes. I'm sorry," said David.

"Now pick up your chair and sit back down, please," said Grandma. She might have been small, but she was tough. She had to be in order to have put up with Grampa all these years. David did as he was told and sat back down.

"Have you calmed down?"

"Yes," replied David. "But why do you want your friend to look at my box?"

"Davie, do you believe in ghosts?" David's eyes narrowed.

"Um... no, not really," he lied. "Why?"

"Well, I believe in things that you might find silly, and I haven't been able to stop thinking about your box since the man at the antique store said that it was haunted."

"Okay, and your friend?"

"She's a medium; someone who's able to communicate with the dead. I have my suspicions that that man wasn't lying."

"Do I have a choice in this?" asked David. Grandma looked evenly at David sitting across from her at the small parfait table, but there was something cold to her look; a detachment had formed.

"Not really. No," replied Grandma. She took a last sip of her now tepid decaf, winced, then got up and walked out of the conservatory, leaving David alone.

8

April 28, 2020

Gordon took a window seat at a small diner that was across the street and a block away from the parking structure where Donny had parked the Mark IV twenty-four hours prior. Although the vantage wasn't ideal, he hoped to at least hear the explosion, and actually, he didn't want to be too close, just in case. It was 12:20 p.m. He ordered a piece of chocolate cream pie and a coffee. His seat faced the structure and if he craned his neck, he could just make it out. He waited. He looked at his watch. He took a refill from the waitress who was friendly and had great legs.

At 1:14 p.m., a tremendous fireball exploded from out of the upper-middle part of the parking structure. The shockwave was immediate. Gordon ducked, sure that the plate glass window he was sitting next to would shatter out of its frame, but it just rattled and shook.

Car alarms wailed up and down the street, people screamed, and in no time scores of police cruisers and emergency vehicles swarmed the street, their hundreds of blinking, red and blue rotating lights and loud sirens transforming the hip urban setting into a surreal terror zone worthy of a Hollywood movie set. Flames continued to lick from the side of the parking structure, but within minutes they were extinguished by the powerful spray of a ladder truck.

The restaurant emptied and patrons, a cook, and two of the waitresses stood on the sidewalk, gawking at the mayhem. But not Gordon. He simply watched from his seat in the diner and gulped down the rest of his coffee. Soon news vans arrived and helicopters hovered and circled over the tragic scene.

Gordon paid his tab and left a generous tip. He walked out the back and hopped into his Eldorado and drove back to the Pointes.

Gordon had hired Joey Lupozinni to take care of Donny, his former fix-it man, and Phyllis's driver for over forty years.

Known in certain circles as Joey "the Loops," he was known to always "loop back" and double check everything he did. He was methodic and no two jobs were ever accomplished in the same way, so it was very difficult for law enforcement to tie one job to the next. Joey "the Loops" was a lone wolf and took care of things singlehandedly: he made sure that the structure's security cameras would go down twenty-four-hours prior to the explosion, and he used an explosive that would minimize structural damage. Above all, Joey "the Loops" made sure that the explosion would take care of Gordon's problem. When Donny opened the trunk of the Mark IV—BOOM! No more Donny.

A couple of days later an FBI agent showed up at the gate on Bishop Street. Gordon was ready. He buzzed him in and they beelined to his office.

"Please take a seat," and, "Drink? Scotch?" and "Of course. I understand, you're on duty."

Gordon was friendly and cooperative.

"The last time I saw him was about a month ago. We were in my garage sitting in the Mark IV I'd sold him."

"Yes, I had a long, professional relationship with Donny."

"No, I wouldn't say we were friends. I mean he had his circle, and I had mine, you know?"

"Mostly we talked about cars. His knowledge of cars was encyclopedic, in fact, he'd go with me whenever I'd make classic car purchases. It's because of Donny that I only have nine classic cars instead of a hundred. He kept me from making a lot of bad and expensive decisions."

"Yeah, mostly he was my wife's chauffeur, but he did a few other things too, errands, odds and ends, and like I said, he helped me with car stuff."

"Oh, and he was an excellent mechanic too. All those cars in my garage, he worked on exclusively. I wouldn't let anyone else touch them. I mean, I already miss his expertise."

"Well yeah, in that he was our chauffeur and mechanic, he had free rein of the garage."

"Donny had come to me with some pretty heavy gambling debts. He asked if I could help out a little, but I told him that my money was tied up and that the best I could do would be to sell him one of my cars, cheap, you know? I gave him a deal to help him out, and he actually picked out the one that he loved the most—my '76 Mark IV."

"As I said, he seemed to have had a gambling problem, and I base that on the fact that he came to me for help."

"I have no idea how much he owed. I didn't ask, and to be honest, I didn't want to know."

"He'd come to me one other time for money, I'm gonna say maybe ten years ago? And I remember telling him to get a handle on it, so yes, I had spoken to him once or twice about his gambling over the years, but it was his life, you know? What was I supposed to do?"

"I thought he'd had a handle on it, up until a month ago when he confided in me that he owed someone a lot of money, and that he was being threatened."

"Take the car," I told him. "Lincolns are pretty hot right now. You should get a pretty penny for it."

"Nope! I have no idea why he didn't sell it; maybe because he loved it? Who knows?"

"I have no idea who his gambling associates were, nor did I want to know. 'I don't want to know, Donny,' I'd say to him."

The agent left his card and told Gordon that if he thought of anything else that could help in the investigation, to not hesitate to get in touch.

9

November 11, 2020: 1:00 p.m.

After blessing and smudging David's room, Annalise took a seat on an old, wood folding chair facing the dowry box. She was tall, thin, and wore her crown of red hair piled high. She wiped her large, round glasses with a cloth, then placed them back onto the bridge of her long, patrician nose. Her demeanor was elegant and her style gravitated toward hippy-chic.

She stared at the beautiful ebony wood dowry box with its inlay and filigree, its vines that snaked and curved upward from the sides and onto the top, and admired the ivory lilies that blossomed open on the lid. There was something familiar about the gold and platinum depiction on the front of the box, that of Salome holding the severed head of John the Baptist on a tray. Although macabre, she recognized the beauty of the Art Nouveau style, and could see how a thirteen-year-old boy would be attracted to this stunning, yet gory work of art. The handles, locking mechanism, and hinges were also high quality, and gleamed in spite of the dim in David's room, the light of a cloudy day filtering in through a small dormer window behind David's bed.

It occurred to Annalise that this was a rather small and spartan room, and she wondered why David had been relegated to the third floor, at the very end of the hall. There were other, much grander bedrooms on the second floor, with fireplaces and ensuite baths, but David was lodged in what used to be servants' quarters.

She'd allowed herself to be distracted by the surroundings, but sometimes distractions could lead to important clues. Sometimes it was the spirit itself that influenced distractions... to deflect and deceive. Annalise cleared her head and zeroed her focus back toward the box. It was obvious that, in its day, the box was an expensive and treasured luxury item... but was there a spirit attachment? She closed her eyes, lifted her arms toward the box, spread her fingers palms down, and began to meditate.

She detected the scent of lilies beginning to infuse the atmosphere in the small room. *Yes, talk to me,* she thought. A series of sepia-toned images flashed in her mind's eye, like looking at an old album filled with cracked daguerreotypes: an unhappy bride alone at the altar; a feminine hand, nails buffed to a shine, and blood dripping from the ring finger; blood-soaked hands holding a bloody dagger; an old woman in a tattered and stained wedding gown. And now a vision of the dowry box opening, and in turn revealing a dark, bottomless pit. Raw emotions came rushing from the box toward Annalise and she had to be careful to not analyze but to simply allow them to be. Sitting in the chair, she felt a litany of intense feelings: betrayal; pain; hate; betrayal; despair; unimaginable sorrow; hate; envy; panic; betrayal; revenge... revenge... revenge.

The scent of lilies became putrid, and the temperature in the room plummeted. Annalise kept her eyes closed and continued to meditate in spite of the manifestation of these unpleasant phenomena. *What are you telling me?* thought Annalise.

The dowry box's lid flew open, and smacked against the wall behind it, sounding like a gallows door swinging open. Startled from her meditation, Annalise opened her eyes and fell backward off the folding chair when she saw a haggard woman in a tea-stained wedding gown swinging by a rope above the box, her white eyes staring hatefully down at Annalise.

"I know what you are now. You have no power over me," said Annalise.

November 11, 2020: 2:00 p.m.

Phyllis and Annalise sat facing each other in high-back armchairs while a fire roared in the large library fireplace. In spite of the coziness, Annalise could not shake the chill of the apparition in David's room.

Phyllis poured some hot, loose tea for Annalise and herself, then gently pushed a small plate of shortbread cookies toward her guest on the small antique table between them.

"These cookies are from an English bakery in the village. Try one, they're delightful," said Phyllis. Annalise took a cookie and placed it on her plate. Her hand trembled slightly.

"Thank you," said Annalise.

"I have to admit I'm on pins and needles, and I'm dying to know how it went," said Phyllis. Annalise took a sip of her tea, then gave her cup a quick swirl and placed it back onto the saucer. Bits of tea leaves swirled in the vortex.

"First, I'd like to ask you some questions about the box," said Annalise.

"Sure."

"When and how did the box come into your possession?"

"Let me think," began Phyllis. "Oh yes, it was on Halloween actually. Gordon and I enjoy going on what we call junking excursions, you know, perusing antique shops and whatnot. I remember because we were supposed to take David, our grandson, to his friend's house to go trick-or-treating, but time just got away from us, so... you know how these things happen."

"So you bought it from an antique shop?"

"Yes. Many of the furnishings and bric-a-brac in our home have come from antique shops, auctions, estate sales, and what-not." Annalise nodded and brushed a stray lock of red hair from her forehead and took another sip of tea, and once again gave her cup a quick swirl. Phyllis continued:

"I've been having some very strange and lucid dreams that I'm dancing with my old ballroom dance partner, but they're so real," said Phyllis. She took a bite of her cookie and a sip of her tea. A log in the fireplace popped and a few embers struck the grate, startling Annalise.

"Don't tell me anything else," said Annalise.

Phyllis noticed the agitation in her friend's usually calm demeanor. "Is everything okay?"

"No, Phyllis. Everything is not okay."

"Why? What happened up there?"

"I don't want to upset you, but you have got to get that box out of your house today, and the sooner the better, like, call the movers right now!"

"Okay, now you're scaring me."

"Phyllis, you should be scared, so I'm just going to come out and say it: I believe that dowry box is possessed by a soul collector," said Annalise. "A very powerful and malevolent entity." Annalise took the last sip of her tea and gave it a swirl. She watched the bits of leaves form into the shape of a cross with a circle around it. Phyllis saw Annalise's reaction as she looked into her cup.

"What are you seeing in the leaves?"

"A cross encircled: entrapment. It fits," said Annalise. Her anxiety ratcheted. She stood suddenly and walked toward the fireplace. "Do you feel the chill in here?"

"No."

"You told me that you've been having lucid dreams about your dance partner. Is he deceased?"

"Tommy? Yes. He died over forty years ago. And his death was so... very unexpected. Sudden."

"And these dreams started after the box was brought into your home?"

"Yes."

"Now this is important: in life, did you and Tommy love each other?" Phyllis averted the intensity of Annalise's gaze and looked down into her cup of tea.

"I'm going to tell you something very personal, okay?"

"I know that this isn't easy," said Annalise, walking toward Phyllis. She crouched and cupped Phyllis's hands. "Please know that you have my complete discretion."

"Tommy and I had an affair that resulted in a child — my son Alex, David's father. He and his wife were killed in a car accident in March. I actually loved Tommy very much," said Phyllis. "And God help me, I still do." Annalise turned and walked away, her hands now clasped in deep thought. She turned and sat on the arm of a sofa facing Phyllis.

"Tommy has passed on but a part of him never left your side." Annalise noted the confusion in Phyllis, and clarified. "What I mean is, Tommy is attached to you, and normally that's not a bad thing, but here's the part that *is* bad: Tommy is being used by the soul collector... it collects the dead, but craves the living. It won't stop until everyone under this roof is dead."

"This is very frightening and I don't want to hear anymore," said Phyllis.

Annalise stared at Phyllis then turned suddenly and stared at the doorway. What she saw confirmed her gifts. And what she saw terrified her.

"Murdered souls are attached to their murderers too! Oh! the souls trapped here! There are many!"

"Please stop! You're frightening me!" shouted Phyllis.

"Your dreams of dancing with Tommy? They're not dreams!" Annalise continued staring at the doorway, her eyes laden in fear.

"Please stop," said Phyllis.

"Have you seen others?"

"I... what?"

"Spirits?"

"Yes," said Phyllis.

"Flowers? Lilies?"

"Yes."

"Phyllis, that box has got to go! Today!"

"And David? My grandson? It's actually his box. We bought it for him."

"Keep him away! Don't let him anywhere near his room until it's gone," said Annalise.

"He's not going to like this. He's become very attached to it."

"How?"

"When I told him that I'd invited you to look at it, he got very angry."

"Then it's already got a strong hold on him. Do everything you can to keep him away from it."

"I'll try."

"You don't understand! Get it out of here!" said Annalise. "My coat? Please? I need to leave."

November 11, 2020: 5:30 p.m.

At dinner Phyllis told Gordon everything that Annalise had said to her about the dowry box. He listened, amused.

"I think it's funny that you believe in all that haunted furniture nonsense," said Gordon. "But that's okay. It just means that I can sell it now. I'd been thinking about it anyway, so I guess you're giving me a green light, huh?" Phyllis looked away troubled, knowing how badly David would take this turn of events.

"Davie is not going to like this one bit. He really loves that box."

"And a month from now he'll be throwing his dirty skivvies on top of it. Trust me, he'll get over it," said Gordon. "Kids, especially teenagers, always get bored and move on to the next bright and shiny thing. Trust me."

"Maybe you're right. But Annalise did say that we need to get it out of the house now! Like, right now! Tonight!"

"Do you know what time it is? That's not going to happen. And I think we'll live through one more night with the scary box in the house. Don't worry about it."

"Well, I don't want Davie sleeping up there tonight."

"He'll be fine. Don't be such a worrywart! And where is he by the way?"

"Do you remember on Halloween how he wanted us to drop him off at his friend's house?" said Phyllis. Gordon nodded while helping himself to more mashed potatoes. "Well, that friend of his was hit by a car and killed, so Davie's at the cemetery paying his respects."

"Hmm... that's too bad. Pass the gravy, would you?"

10

November 11, 2020: 5:30 p.m.

A rectangular mound of dirt covered the fresh grave, which was in turn covered by a blanket of artificial grass. There were hundreds of flowers strewn on and around the grave, and a few wet stuffed animals lay around the grave too. A temporary marker identified the grave as Zach's, and somehow it all looked so cheap and tawdry. This is not how David wanted to remember his best friend.

"Hey Zach. First off, you gotta know that I would have been there on Halloween if I could have, you know that. But my grampa is a giant asshole, and he wouldn't drive me to your house that night. And it's not like we were even that far away. All they want to do is go to boring antique shops and spend hours looking at old, crappy, shit. Seriously, I hate him. My grandma is nice, but she can be pretty clueless too. Sometimes things are cool with her, and other times she's cold as ice, so I never know where I stand with her. And just so you know, I hate Townsend. I already got in trouble and got suspended, and I had to write a stupid paper to get back in, but at least going to school gets me out of that house."

David looked up and around. Some of the headstones were huge, old, towering things: a tall obelisk with the name on the base, weathered and difficult to read. A giant granite scroll with the family name of Schmidt carved into the scroll, and the names of everyone buried underneath. A shiny, black granite bench with Stottmeyer carved into the side of it. David looked back at

Zach's grave but there wasn't anything to it to even remotely connect David with his best friend—just a cold pile of dirt covered by fake grass, flowers, and wet stuffed animals.

"I'm sorry," said David, his eyelids welling with tears. He looked up at the sky and saw two kites flying off in the distance and the tears started to flow. "You were my best friend. I want you to know that, and I can't believe you're gone. Please don't think I'm weird for saying this, but..." David looked off toward a grouping of shrubs and trees with tears flowing. "I love you. I love you like a brother. I never had a brother, but you are my brother, I want you to know that, and I'm so, so, so sorry. I miss you so much. First my parents, and now you. I don't know how I'm supposed to deal with this shit. Seriously, Zach! What am I gonna do?" His question was met with silence, and as the wind gusted through bare tree branches, a plastic baggie skittered across the brown turf of the cemetery. Further off an old, heavy-set woman knelt at a grave with grass clippers. David looked around at Zach's new surroundings and he was disgusted on behalf of his friend.

"This is lame, bro... I'm glad you can't see it, because you would hate it. Oh, and if you ever visit me again, try not to scare the shit out of me, okay?"

It was getting darker and David regretted destroying his phone. He wouldn't be able to Uber back to his grandparent's house.

"Damn. I've never taken the bus before, and now I gotta figure that out. Oh well... wish me luck," said David. "Oh, and I just want you to know... I'm never coming back here again. This isn't how I want to remember you. You're better than this place Zach, and I want to remember you in my heart."

11

November 11, 2020: 6:00 p.m.

Phyllis opened the junk drawer in the butler's pantry and searched for the keys to the rooms on the third floor. Instead of arguing with David, she'd tell him a harmless, white lie that she practiced as she looked for the keys:

"Davie I'm sorry, but the cleaning lady was upstairs and saw termites, so we had to have the rooms fumigated. No one can go up there for forty-eight hours. I hope you don't mind, but I brought all your stuff to a second-floor bedroom—the yellow room! It's more comfortable anyway, I think you'll like it."

Phyllis finally found the keys. They were old, steel, skeleton keys all looped on an iron ring. She huffed it up to the third floor and walked the length of the long, dark hallway, locking each door as she passed each room. She reached the end of the hall and stopped at David's room. She put her ear close to the door and listened but heard nothing. She knocked, waited, then went in.

The room was smaller than she remembered, and as she looked around, she was embarrassed that she'd allowed Gordon to put David in such a shabby, small room. Even on the brightest and sunniest days, the light coming in through the small dormer window was inadequate. She looked at the dowry box sitting on the opposite wall. It just sat there, minding its own business...

waiting. Phyllis opened the small dresser and shoved David's clothing—his socks, underwear, jeans, tee-shirts, dress shirts and pants, his pajamas, slippers, and shoes—into a large laundry basket, picked it up, then carried it out of the room, locking the door behind her. She thought she heard something on the other side of the door... like a lid creaking open. She hurried down the hallway toward the double-winder staircase, carefully descended, then made her way down the hall to David's new room. She placed the large laundry basket onto an old hope chest at the foot of the queen-size bed. "Whew!" she said. "I think he'll like this room better than that old, dark, drafty room up there. This is much cozier."

12

November 11, 2020: 11:00 p.m.

Phyllis paced nervously in her bedroom. The gilt clock on her mantel read that it was eleven, and David was still not back from the cemetery. It was a school night, and this was very out of character for him.

"It's eleven-o-clock and Davie's not home yet and I'm worried," she said. "I wish he'd call."

"How's he supposed to call? I've still got his cellphone," shouted Gordon from his room.

"I thought you gave it back to him?"

"I didn't give it back to him! It's still locked in the glove compartment of the Fleetwood, or at least it better be!" said Gordon. He walked into Phyllis's room and peeked out of a window that offered a vantage of the garage where a light was on. "Goddammit!"

"What's the matter?" said Phyllis.

"I think your precious grandson is snooping around in my garage!"

"What?"

"There's a light on in the garage! I'm going down there!"

"Go easy on him, Gordon. I'm sure there's a good explanation."

"Yeah, right... that's exactly what I'll do... I'll go easy on him, Phyllis, don't worry."

"Gordon! I mean it!"

Gordon put on a windbreaker and walked out through the *port cochere* door and trounced the two-hundred feet toward his garage. He tried the door but it was locked.

"Alright, what the hell are you doing in there?" yelled Gordon. "Open up!" He pounded on the door and jiggled the locked handle again, and the door gave way. Gordon had taken a few steps into the garage when the door slammed shut, then locked behind him.

"Very funny, wise guy. What the hell are you doing in my garage?" The lightbulb that had been turned on suddenly exploded with a loud pop, and glass tinkled onto the floor. Blue-tinged cigarette smoke hovered five feet above the concrete.

"Goddammit, kid, this isn't funny! Come out from where you're hiding and take your medicine!" said Gordon. The unmistakable sound of a Zippo snapping open and the thumb wheel striking flint emanated through the garage. A cloud of cigarette smoke streamed out from the driver's seat window of the '58 Eldorado Seville—a Concours d'Elegance best of show winner, and the most valuable car by far in Gordon's collection.

"So now you've taken up smoking, huh? Get the fuck out of that car! Now! It's worth more than you can count to!" said Gordon, walking toward his best of show treasure, but then the car door opened. Donny, or what was left of him, climbed out of the old Caddy. A cigarette was clenched between his teeth being that his lips were no longer a part of his face. An eye dangled from its socket, and his right arm was gone below the elbow.

"Got a little surprise for you, Gordo," said Donny. "Remember Toledo Dee? Oh, she's been missin' you somethin' fierce. She's been cryin' about you all night long!"

Gordon couldn't speak. He just stared at the man he'd had killed a few months ago. He felt his heart hammering in his chest as he backed away from the apparition.

"Yeah, good 'ole Toledo Dee. She's been dyin' to see you, so I sez to her, I sez, 'Hop in, Dee. Let's go see Gordo, you know, for old time's sake.'" Donny's stump pointed at something behind Gordon.

"Well, Whaddya know! There she is, right behind you!"

Gordon spun and standing directly in front of him was his old lover Dee, only a little more worse for wear since the last time he'd seen her twenty-five years ago.

"Her landlord unlocked her door and went in after some of her neighbors complained about the rotten stench coming from her place," said Donny, as Dee stumbled closer toward Gordon.

"Yeah, he told me it stunk so bad his eyes were watering by the time he reached the kitchen. And there she was, her body sticking half-way out of the oven. She'd been laying there dead for five days—said she'd blown out the pilot light." Gordon hyperventilated as the stench of natural gas and rotting flesh was making him faint.

"Yeah, they ruled it a suicide, but we know what really happened, don't we, Dee? Don't we, Gordo?"

Just then all nine cars in the garage started, and their engines revved to red-line RPMs. Smoke belched from their exhaust pipes.

"Oh, Gordon," said Dee. "I've missed you, baby! Let me hold you, please." The blue and bloated apparition wrapped its arms around Gordon. He hacked and coughed and was overcome by the deadly cocktail of multiple noxious and deadly fumes.

"I wanna get naughty, Gordon, don't you? Come on baby, hold me. Hold me like I told you to. Hold me just like in the old days, remember?" Gordon's scream was drowned out by the revving of nine very powerful V-8s. Dee squeezed harder and harder as Gordon's eyes rolled upward, and the last thing he saw was a woman in a tea-stained wedding gown staring down at him from the rafters.

November 11, 2020: 11:30 p.m.
Phyllis was relieved that David was home, but not exactly thrilled he was snooping around in Gordon's garage. She'd talk to him about it at breakfast in the morning to make sure that he

knew it's Grampa's garage, and his precious jalopies are his pride and joy, and absolutely no one is allowed in there — period!

She looked at the garage through her bedroom window. The light was no longer on. *Maybe Gordon and Davie are talking it out in one of his cars,* thought Phyllis. *That would be nice. I hope they'll work things out. Maybe tonight's finally the night.*

Phyllis changed into her pajamas, washed her face, then put her kimono on and walked down the hall toward the stairway. She had to tell David her little white lie about the termites, and show him the yellow room, his new digs. He'd have his own bathroom and everything. And he'll still have his privacy because it's way on the other end of the hallway.

Phyllis smelled lilies. Something twinkled in the crystals. Tommy's eyes! She stopped and looked down. Tommy stood under the chandelier looking up at Phyllis. He had that flirty sparkle that she found so irresistible.

"Hello Phyllis. Care to trip the light fantastic? Come on... for old time's sake," said Tommy. His eyes shined, and his lips parted, revealing those beautiful pearly whites. His left arm went behind his back and his right arm extended outward in a graceful and elegant invitation back onto the dance floor.

"Tommy, no. I know what's happening. She has control."

"Phyllis, please. I have to go soon. When the clock strikes twelve... you know the story," said Tommy looking up imploringly at his dance partner and lover. His eyes bewitched, he looked impeccable in his fitted tuxedo, and his shoes were buffed to a high shine.

"It's all for you Phyllis. It's all for you."

Phyllis slowly walked down the curved stairway. Her years of exercise and stretching had paid off, and her comportment, poise, and balance were nearly as great as the last time they'd danced together over forty years ago. The crystals above tinkled sounding like the anticipatory applause that Tommy and Phyllis often received as they'd strike their opening position.

As Phyllis approached Tommy, she lifted her chin, pulled her shoulders back, then executed a perfect double spin, which positioned her directly in front of Tommy. She noticed the rope burn poking out from his collar—if anyone could survive that, it would've been Tommy. The crystals above tinkled their approval as Tommy took Phyllis into his arms, and her back arched gracefully, responding to his lead. And now they danced under the swaying shadow of the large chandelier which spun and rocked on its chain above, mirroring the flawless grace of the dancing pair on the marble floor of the vestibule. The only thing missing was an adoring audience but then Phyllis saw Alex and Madeline looking on in the shadows, *oh, and there's some boy too,* thought Phyllis. *I wonder who that is. He must love ballroom dancing.*

"That's Zach," said Tommy, reading Phyllis. "He's a good egg." Phyllis gave Zach a smile and wink as Tommy spun, then dipped her. Zach's head was gashed and tilted oddly as he glared at the couple dancing under the violently rocking chandelier. Bits of plaster from the ceiling medallion fell onto the floor at their feet. Phyllis's eyes followed her hand as it arched upward in an elegant pose, but what she saw beyond the span of her reach made her scream. The woman in the tea-stained wedding gown jumped from the balustrade and onto the chandelier. The metal chain groaned and gave way, sparks shot from severed wiring, more plaster fell, and the massive, eleven-hundred-pound chandelier collapsed, crushing Phyllis, killing her instantly. Impaled by the shrapnel of hundreds of dagger-sharp shards of crystal, her dark, crimson blood quickly pooled, spreading outward in stark contrast to the white marble of the vestibule floor. Phyllis's dead eyes gazed up toward the thing that killed her.

November 11, 2020: 11:58 p.m.

David was having another horrible day in a string of horrible months since March when he'd gotten the news that his parents had been killed. It had been one disaster after another, and living with his grandparents had proved to be almost unendurable. Sure, Grandma was mostly okay, but she was sometimes removed and cold, and wondering where he stood with her from day to day was exhausting. Grampa was something else entirely. David had no idea what he'd done to deserve his hatred, and no matter how he tried, he couldn't seem to do anything right around him.

Why did Mom and Dad have to die? And Zach? I don't know how I'm going to do this, he thought. *At least I've got my box. She's the only thing that matters right now, and I need her. I need my goddess.* No one would have believed him, and no one would have understood, so it was his secret. *She takes me away... far from everything.*

These and many other thoughts plagued his mind as he walked all the way back to his Grandparents from the cemetery, an almost twenty-mile hike because, as it turned out, he didn't have the money for bus fare, and none of the bus drivers were kind enough to allow him onto their busses, not a single one... so he walked.

Literally everything sucks right now, he thought. He finally reached Bishop Street, walked another half-mile, and arrived at the gate of his grandparent's estate. He looked left, then right, then mounted and climbed over the six-foot high gate with the spear finials.

David walked the length of the curved blacktop driveway and up ahead saw something strange: smoke was pouring out of the garage from under the eaves and soffits. He ran toward it thinking that there might be a fire. He peeked in through a window. Before his eyes adjusted to the darkness, he heard motors revving and racing, then he saw smoke puking from every car's exhaust pipe. He looked further to the right and saw Grampa laying on the floor. His eyes were wide open, and a nasty, greenish snot foamed from out of his mouth and nose. David stood there for a few minutes staring at his grandfather. He never moved a muscle. He was dead.

Finally... something good, thought David.

Although he'd never admit it to Grandma, he was actually relieved that Grampa was dead. Of course he would be there for her, but he'd keep his true feelings to himself. He walked from the garage and toward the house in no particular hurry. *He's dead anyway... what's the rush?*

The *port cochere* door was open, so he walked through it and into the pantry, through the kitchen, down the hall, and into the vestibule.

He stopped.

Grandmother was lying dead in a large and growing pool of blood, crushed under the huge chandelier that had fallen on top of her. Chunks of shattered plaster and broken crystals littered the floor. *Oh my God!* thought David. A deep sense of panic crept up his spine as he looked down at his poor grandmother. *But how?* This was so shocking that it couldn't be processed. *They're both dead! This doesn't make any sense. How is this possible?*

He crouched down closer to her face. Her wide-open eyes stared blankly toward the ceiling.

"Grandma, can you hear me?" he asked. There was no reply. She was dead. *But how is it that Grampa is dead in the garage, and Grandma is dead here under the chandelier?*

"How can this be?" he said. "This doesn't make any sense."

This was such an unbelievable shock, and there wasn't any time to process it. Just like when his counselor at Bromley, Mrs. Lewis, told him that his parents had been killed, he remembered how numb he felt. The sorrow and tears actually took a few hours to catch up, and he was finally able to cry over his parents in the small room at the end of the hall on the third floor.

My goddess. I need my goddess, he thought. Then something snapped. It was all too much to bear, and the voices of the dead began swirling and calling out.

"Hey, David!" said a voice from somewhere down the hall.

"Zach?" said David. "Is that you?"

"Hey, son!" another voice from where? The kitchen? David's head whipped around toward the voice.

"Dad? Where are you?" He stood and took one last look at Grandma. Her face was turning blue.

"David, we've been missing you! Let's get going, we haven't got much time." Mom's voice! Was she upstairs?

"Mom? Where are you?" said David. He walked toward the stairway and looked up. He checked every room on the first floor and followed the voices — the library, the conservatory, the kitchen, Grandma's dance studio. But he couldn't find them.

"Come on! Where are you guys? Stop playing!" said David, happy to hear them, but frustrated that they wouldn't come out from their hiding places.

"Trick-or-treat! Trick-or-treat!" said Zach.

"Wait up, Zach!" said David.

David bounded up the curved stairway two treads at a time and walked the length of the second floor, peeking into each room, but found nothing and no one.

"Where you guys at?"

"We're here!" said Dad.

"Give me something good to eat!"

"Wait up! I'm coming!" David trounced up the narrow stairway to the third floor. He snapped on the hallway light, obliterating the black. Zach stood at the other end of the hallway next to David's bedroom door. He looked at David, his head tilted oddly, and the deep gash still visible.

"Hello, David," said Zach. "Let's go."

David stopped and looked at his dead friend.

"Zach, I'm scared."

"Trick-or-treat," said Zach. "Give me something good to eat."

"I don't have a costume," said David.

"It's okay."

Zach dashed into David's room.

"Hey Zach, wait up! I'm coming!" David ran down the length of the hallway and into his room. The dowry box's lid was open.

"We're all here," said Zach.

"Come on, son!" said Dad.

"Let's get a move on, David," said Mother. "We don't want to be late."

David looked into the darkness inside the box. He heard whispers, chattering... and was someone crying?

"I'm scared," said David, staring into the infinite dark.

"Hurry, or we'll leave without you!"

David stepped into the box and disappeared into its black depths.

The lid slammed shut and the dowry box locked. Then it began to transform. The shiny, ebony wood began to fade and dry rot. The filigreed vines and ivory lilies dulled. The brightwork, the locks, hinges, and handles tarnished and oxidized to a bluish-black, and the gold and platinum depiction of Salome holding the head of John the Baptist disappeared under a hundred years of age, silt, and grime.

David was never seen again.

EPILOGUE

September 22, 2024

After a few years of the property being tied up in probate, Bostwick, Spellman, & James had been hired to manage the estate sale at 32 Bishop Street in Grosse Pointe Shores. The proceeds from the sale would be divided up between certain charities that Phyllis Price supported, and a scholarship would be endowed in the memory of Gordon Price. Their grandson David had still not been found, and was considered a missing person.

Over two-hundred cars lined Bishop and the adjacent streets. The catalogue of items had been posted online; there were over one-hundred pages and the lots ran into the thousands. Many people came for the promise of great antiques, but many others came because of the notorious and tragic circumstances surrounding the deaths of the former owners—Gordon and Phyllis Price.

Marsha Spellman, one of the owners of the company managing the estate sale, was on the second floor attending a register when a strange man walked up to her. He was thin and slight with bad posture, and seemed weighed down by the thick, brown, craftsman's leather apron he wore.

"Excuse me, ma'am?"

Marsha looked up from her work and noticed the strange man and smiled.

"Yes sir, how can I help you?"

The man nervously ran his fingers through his comb-over.

"Well, up on the third floor, at the end of the hall, there's a box I'm interested in. I believe it's a dowry box, or maybe an old hope chest?"

"Oh yes! That old, ugly box up there. Honestly I didn't bother putting a price tag on it because I was sure it wouldn't sell. Are you interested?"

"Yes. I'm fairly good with my hands. Maybe I can clean it up a little and whatnot. Anyway, what are you asking for it?"

"Would you be willing to pay twenty-five dollars for it?"

"Yes, that's fair, said Mr. Hintermann, taking his billfold from the pocket in his leather vest.

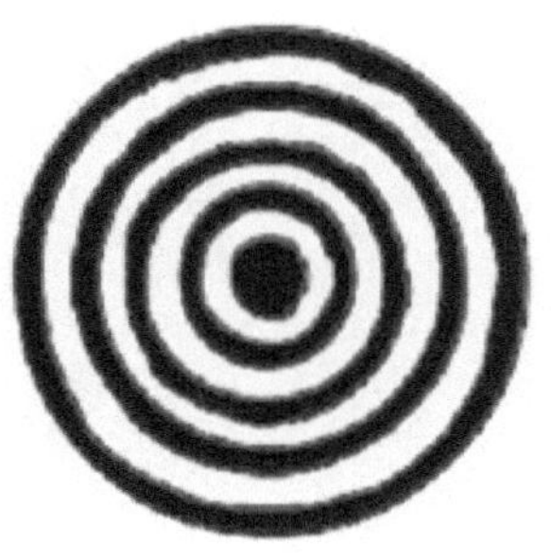

THE DYBBUK'S CURSE

Donald Levin

One day you will do things for me that you hate.
That is what it means to be a family.

           —Jonathan Safran Foer,
           Everything is Illuminated

1

The second she walked in I knew she was in the wrong place.

She looked more like the kind of client television detectives handle—mid-thirties, I judged, long blonde hair, hard-shine manicure, legs up to the proverbial "there"… And in fact, she wanted what most people want when they think about hiring a private investigator: she needed someone to trail her husband. She reckoned he was getting too chummy with his massage therapist (according to her, a comely Norwegian named Astrid) and wanted me to find out if there was any funny business going on between them. Pretty standard case for this line of work. You followed somebody around, sooner or later caught them in a compromising position, took some photos—then washed the sleaze off at the end of the day with a long, hot shower.

Except I didn't take those kinds of jobs.

"We all specialize in different things," I told her. "I just don't happen to solve these kinds of problems for people. But lots of others do. Here." I opened my desk drawer and took out a card for the firm down the hall. DesJardins Investigations. I handed it to her and said, "You might find them more appropriate for what you want." This kind of case was Pete DesJardins's bread and butter; I knew they would be perfect for each other.

The way things turned out, I wished I had taken on her case after all and turned away the next client who came through my door.

2

For the next few hours, I was alone in the office. Halloween was typically a busy day for me, but this one was unusually quiet for some reason. Part of the problem was, I didn't have a secretary. Sadly, I always seemed to be without a secretary... not everybody wanted to work for an agency like mine. When people hear I run a one-man paranormal detective agency, they immediately start humming the theme from "Ghostbusters," like I'm out there with a fifty-pound ghost-sucker on my back making the city safe from ghouls. In fact, most of my work winds up *disproving* paranormal events—Aunt Sadie isn't really haunting the attic, it's just a raccoon; Uncle Wilbur didn't really turn into a werewolf, that's just coyote scat in your backyard, and so on. I do find genuine paranormal events, of course, but they're not as prevalent as you might think. I'm more of a researcher than a ghost buster. I try to explain away hauntings and other phenomena, and when I find evidence that points to a genuine paranormal episode, I'll meet with the client to decide what the best course of action is. I typically don't do exterminations or exorcisms—that's a whole other specialty.

The other problem with finding a secretary was, tell a job applicant you're a private investigator and they assume you're some hardboiled tough guy who thinks with his fists and spends the days and nights soused. Either that or they expect you to make a pass at them, because isn't it *de rigueur* for the secretary to have intimate relations with the shamus? You can blame TV and the movies for that, too. I had to tell some good candidates that I was one of those ethical detectives you don't hear much about; I didn't fool around with the help, and in general, I was the quiet type; you could have even called me scholarly... wouldn't hurt a fly. That discouraged a lot of people who wanted the adventure.

So in the absence of any new business on that quiet Halloween, I puttered around the office for a few hours, feeding the circular file with junk mail, paying bills, and finishing up final reports for a few clients: a pair of genuine hauntings and a couple more false alarms.

When the elementary school down the street let out in the afternoon, the kids came treat-or-treating in my office building with their moms, as they've done every year. I used to put a bowl of candy for them outside my door so they wouldn't bother me constantly, but every year one of the little buggers would dump the whole bowl into his bag so I stopped that. Now I just prop the door open and let them come in to take the candy I hand out. Anyway, it's fun to see them troop in and out in their costumes—the little girls in princess outfits with the occasional Wonder Woman, and the little boys all in touch with their inner macho superheroes. I also get a kick out of the makeup on the little Wolfmen and Draculas—especially since I know some werewolves and vampires personally and they don't look anything like their movie counterparts, which is what the little kids always imitate.

After the little ones left, I heard a knock on the outside office door. I called, "Come in."

The door opened and a woman who looked to be in her late seventies entered my inner sanctum. She was short and painfully thin with a pale, drawn face, deep smudged circles under her eyes, and a paisley bandana knotted around her head. She entered tentatively. I could tell right away she was a sick woman. Still, she was more like what I was used to than my earlier visitor. Younger people tend not to believe in paranormal episodes, and if they do they're more likely to welcome them than hire an investigator like me to root them out.

"Are you Mr. McGillis?" she asked.

"I am."

The name of the firm is McGillis and Associates, Confidential Investigations. I don't have associates, but the fancy title makes the company sound like it's more than a lone wolf baying at the moon. Plus I like to stay away from anything "paranormal" in the agency name; it tends to bring out the kooks, and I see enough of those as it is. I never advertise. My business comes exclusively through word-of-mouth.

I said, "And you are—?"

"Sarah Friedman. Pleased to meet you."

She approached with her hand out. I shook it—her hand was ice-cold and all bones—and invited her to sit in the chair on the opposite side of my desk.

"What can I do for you, Mrs. Friedman?"

"Please, call me Sarah."

"Sarah, then. How can I help?"

"I understand you're a private detective who specializes in the supernatural?"

"Correct."

"I would like to hire your services."

"How did you hear about me?"

"You were recommended by a certain individual whom I'd rather not name."

"Fair enough." Some people are embarrassed at the thought of seeking a paranormal investigator and don't want it bruited about. "My fee is $150 an hour with a $600 minimum, plus expenses. I cost more than the usual detective agency because of the uncommon nature of my work."

"Sounds reasonable."

She opened her pocketbook with a click and withdrew six c-notes. She laid them on my desk. "It shouldn't take you longer than today, so I think this should do it."

I left the bills on the desk. "Mrs. Friedman—Sarah. Before I take your money, let's talk about what you want me to do for you."

"For that, Mr. McGillis, I'll have to tell you a story. It's essential you hear it before we talk about what I have in mind."

"If we're on a first-name basis, please call me Maurice."

"Maurice, may I tell you my story? Do you have time?"

I collected the money and stashed it in my desk drawer. "You just bought my time. I'm all ears."

She settled back in her chair. "It begins a long time ago in a shtetl in Poland," she said, "in the middle of the seventeenth century. You know what a shtetl is?"

"A small Jewish village."

"Yes. At that time, King Charles of Sweden was waging a brutal war of conquest against Poland and the Polish people. It was a war that saw almost a third of the Polish Commonwealth population—three million people—wiped out. In that group were roughly 500,000 Jews, whom Charles treated with particular brutality. Prior to that, with some interruptions, Poland had gained a reputation as a haven for Jews expelled from other countries in Europe. That ended with the Swedish King Charles.

"During Charles's war, there were two Jewish friends from the same shtetl who had been drafted into the Polish army. Their names were Chaim Rosenthal and Shmuel Silberberg. The two men formed an even closer friendship under fire—a brotherhood of arms, the way things will go during wartime.

"As it happened, both of their wives back home in their village were pregnant. The two men made a pact: if one wife gave birth to a son and the other a daughter, the children would wed. In those days, you see, arranged marriages were common, not like today, when people expect to marry for love. Marriages were arranged by parents or by special matchmakers based on political or economic considerations.

"I point this out," Sarah interrupted her tale, "because this has a particular bearing on where my story is going."

I opened my hands, inviting her to continue.

"As the wartime fates would have it, Chaim Rosenthal was killed in one of the final battles when King Charles was trying to occupy Warsaw. His friend Shmuel Silberberg survived the war and returned to their shtetl, where he discovered that their two wives had indeed given birth. Sadly, Shmuel's wife, Golda, died giving birth to their daughter, Leah. Chaim's wife—now his widow, Deborah—gave birth to a boy whom she named Ezra.

"Neither Shmuel nor Deborah ever remarried. Shmuel became a merchant, like his father, and turned into one of the richest men in their village. Ezra's mother Deborah, on the other hand, was poverty-stricken. She became a seamstress and laundress but she had to rely mostly on the charity of the villagers for her and her son's sustenance. But Ezra was a bright boy, and it wasn't long before the village rabbi took an interest in his welfare and arranged for him to attend the local Yeshiva, the religious school, where he excelled in his studies.

"The two children, Ezra and Leah, were brought up like brother and sister; they were inseparable, and as they grew and matured, they fell in love. Their devotion to each other was plain for everyone to see—everyone except Shmuel, that is, who spent too much time counting his *złotys*—his money—and not enough time with his daughter.

"When they reached marriageable age, Leah and Ezra wanted to marry. Neither of them knew that her father Shmuel was secretly negotiating to give Leah's hand in marriage to the son of another wealthy merchant who lived in a nearby village. Shmuel was determined that his daughter would not marry a poor man, especially a penniless student. When he told her about arranging her marriage, Leah begged her father to reconsider and allow her to marry Ezra, the boy she loved. Her father refused, breaking his daughter's heart along with the agreement he had made with Ezra's late father during the war.

"The two young lovers were devastated. Ezra himself went to Shmuel to plead for his daughter's hand in marriage. But Shmuel Silberberg laughed the poor scholar out of his store. In his anguish, the young man turned to the evil and impure forces of the Kabbalah to try to change Shmuel's mind and win back Leah's hand. In a flash, Ezra went from being a good Yeshiva *bocher*—a pious young student of the Torah—to being a devotee of the calamitous negative spirits that he set loose. Those evil spirits soon claimed his life. And in death they tainted his own spirit even more.

"Leah was inconsolable. But the marriage her father arranged went forth regardless. During the wedding ceremony, Leah's betrothed lifted her veil to kiss her and she shrank from him—she couldn't bear to have him touch her, such was the love she still bore for Ezra. When she began her married life with her new husband, she refused to let him put a hand on her, let alone consummate the marriage. Her love for Ezra was still too strong; it ruled her life.

"One night, in the extremity of her grief, Leah snuck away and visited Ezra's grave and threw herself on his headstone and wailed and wailed for Ezra to return. Suddenly she quieted down, and her anguish turned to ecstasy. Ezra did return, in the form of a dybbuk that possessed her."

Here she paused again in her story. "Excuse me for asking, but are you Jewish? With a name like Maurice McGillis, I'm not so sure."

"To be perfectly honest, I'm not sure, either. I never knew my father, and my mother died giving birth to me. I was raised by a loving family who didn't have any particular religious affiliation beyond vague Protestantism—so what I was originally, I just can't say. My origins are a bit mysterious."

"Perhaps that helped determine your current occupation?"

I smiled. "Perhaps. But I hold to no religious beliefs. If anything, I'm a rationalist. But don't worry. I'm well-versed in a variety of religious supernatural traditions, including yours."

"Then you know what a dybbuk is?"

"I do. A soul that dies before its time that returns to earth to complete the task it has left undone and experience the joys and pleasures it has missed."

"Just so," Sarah said, "or, if it's a negative spirit, it returns to cause havoc among those who angered it in life. And now we're getting to the heart of my story."

She continued:

"The rabbis held multiple exorcisms for Leah, complete with the required black candles and rabbinical prayers, but the dybbuk of her dead lover would not leave her. Finally, not wanting to be separated from her dead lover's spirit but tired of being the object of continual exorcisms, she lied to her new husband that the dybbuk had left her, and they began their life together. In the meantime, with Ezra's spirit still possessing her, she became ravenous for sex. She couldn't have sex with Ezra, so she turned to her husband. She couldn't get enough of sex with him. But she knew that her sudden sexual awakening was the expression of her love for her lover's spirit that had joined with hers and had nothing to do with her husband.

"In fact, the dybbuk didn't leave, not just then, anyway. The two lovers merged their spirits. You might think that's the end of our story—but it's only the beginning. After a while, Leah and her husband had twins, a girl and a boy. As her children came of age at thirteen—the age when we consider Jewish children to become adults—the dybbuk finally left Leah, but only because it possessed her son. Legend has it that the spirit-possessed son murdered Leah's father, Shmuel Silberberg, in revenge for forbidding his daughter's marriage to the boy she loved. And when Leah's son grew up and got married, he and *his* wife had two children, a girl and a boy. And it came to pass *that* boy was possessed by the spirit of Ezra when *he* turned thirteen.

"So it went, down through the ages. In each generation, a possessed male had, in his turn, two children, a boy and a girl, where the boy was possessed by the evil spirit of Ezra when he turned thirteen. Ezra's evil dybbuk has traveled down the generations to this day. And it now possesses my grandson, Barry, who turned twenty-one this year."

"Why did it only possess the male of the line?"

"To ensure its own continuation it kept reproducing itself as a male, as the males were more susceptible to its evil influences than the females. As it traveled down through the generations from seventeenth century Poland, Ezra's spirit became more purely evil. From a shadow of evil at first—the kind of evil that would lead Ezra to possess another man's wife, and block her love for her husband—that negative spirit has increased age by age as its thirst for vengeance has grown. It has mostly been kept in check, primarily through the eruption of other energies, including sex. But on one night of the year—Halloween—the spirit of Ezra breaks out of its restraints and compels its host to commit a terrible act of violence."

"Why tonight?" I asked. "Halloween is a Christian holiday, nothing to do with Jews."

"The traditions of Halloween are even older than Christianity. On that night, the fragile tissue between this world and the next is thinnest, and when evil roams the earth generally. Jews don't believe in Satan as the devil, the embodiment of evil; Satan was adopted from the Old Testament into the New Testament and given shape as the devil. Satan in the Old Testament represents the *tendency* toward evil, toward darkness, toward negative actions, as essential to life as goodness. On this night more than any other night, the tendency toward evil is strongest in a spirit that has grown more evil over time, and our abilities to resist are weakest."

Here she paused again.

"Well," I said, "that's quite a tale. But I don't do exorcisms, so I don't know how I can help you."

"I don't want you to do an exorcism," Sarah said. "I want you to find my grandson who is possessed by the ancient spirit of Ezra."

"And then what?"

"And then I want you to kill him."

3

That took me a few moments to recover from. "Surely you mean you want me to kill Ezra's spirit and not the young man himself," I tried to clarify.

"No, I want you to kill Ezra himself. Every year since he became a man at thirteen, the spirit has compelled him to commit an act of violence on Halloween. Every year we tried to restrain him, but the taste for violence had grown too strong—the past few years, he foiled all our efforts to control him. And throughout history, the violence increased in intensity as those young men got older. In my grandson's twenty-first year, the history of the curse is clear: the act will be the ultimate act of violence, the murder of an innocent. As always, his victim must be a Jew."

"Why a Jew?"

"To continue enacting revenge against the man who originally ruined his life, Shmuel Silberberg."

"But why do this now, after all the generations of transmigration of the dybbuk's spirit down through the male bloodline? What's happened that makes you need to stop this tonight?"

"I've thought about this for years, wondering what I'd do when the time came for the curse to express itself in my grandson. Before now I've done nothing. Now I'm an old woman," Sarah said. "I'm riddled with cancer. I won't live to see another Halloween. This abomination has been going on in our family for four hundred years. I can't go to my grave knowing I did nothing to stop it—not when I could have saved who knows how many innocent lives in the future. Especially the one whose life will end tonight by the hand of my grandson."

"Why such an extreme solution? I mean, we're talking about your *grandson*. Why not try another exorcism? As you've said, your religion has a special exorcism ceremony for dybbuks."

"From the beginning, the spirit of Ezra has resisted all exorcisms, down through the generations. In fact, they have only made the dybbuk stronger."

"Sarah, you're asking me to kill your own grandson." It was more a statement than a question; I wanted to make absolutely sure what she was asking me to do.

"That's the only permanent solution," Sarah said.

"If the dybbuk leaves the male host and enters the male child, why have they kept having children? Why haven't they just ended the line?"

"Because the dybbuk is too strong, you see. It takes control. Like a virus, it insists on procreation to prolong its own existence. And it will only continue when it possesses a member of our family. Don't you have the heart for this, Maurice?

Because if you don't, I'll take my money back and go somewhere else."

"Well," I said, "murder is not something I'm called upon to commit as a paranormal investigator. Theoretically, it is one of the services I can offer in the right circumstances."

And I would be saving an innocent life, I thought. But I couldn't just kill Barry Friedman because this woman asked me to; I'd need proof of the dybbuk's possession beyond his grandmother's word. And even then, I'd need compelling evidence her grandson needed to die.

I decided not to mention this. "You said you need me to find your grandson?" I asked instead.

"That's the other problem: I don't know where he is. You'll need to locate him before midnight."

I asked her for a picture of the young man. "You won't need it," she said, "because I'll be coming with you."

"Sarah, this is not something you want to do. You won't want to be there for what's going to happen."

"I have to come with you. I'm not going to ask you to sacrifice my flesh and blood while I'm staying home handing out candy to six-year-olds."

She was adamant—I could see where the family dybbuk got its tenacity—and we started out. It was already six o'clock in the evening—time was getting short. Who knew if we were too late already? Maybe her grandson's dybbuk had already claimed its Halloween victim.

First I unlocked my handgun and holster from the gun safe, and strapped them on my belt. I grabbed the pouch with the vial of holy water and a small crucifix that I always carried with me, and I shoved it in my pocket; I knew they would be useless against this particular spirit, but I'd feel naked without them. Force of habit, I guess.

I drove us in my old Plymouth Barracuda. She directed me to Barry's apartment in a high-rise downtown near the university. Sarah explained that Barry was a graduate student in the university's theatre program. He was engaged to be married to a woman in his program, and that was the other cause for urgency—Sarah wanted to end this curse before Ezra's dybbuk moved into yet another generation.

There was no answer at Barry's, so Sarah called her son's house in the northern suburbs. No answer. "They must be outside handing out candy," she suggested. We were moving into prime trick-or-treat hours.

We drove straight out Woodward to Bloomfield Hills, the wealthy area where Barry's family lived. On the way, Sarah filled me in on what had happened with Barry's father—her son—when he was a younger man.

"Starting when he was thirteen, we locked him in his room on Halloween so he wouldn't have the opportunity for the family curse to work through him. But he went to medical school at the University of Chicago, and there wasn't any chance to protect him or any innocents who might be around him. We begged him to come home for Halloween where we could watch him, but he said he was too busy with his studies. We hoped working in a hospital as he did, doing good works, would mitigate the dybbuk's curse, but we were wrong. He got off shift at nine o'clock on the Halloween after he turned twenty-one and went prowling in downtown Chicago. I told you the spirit is too strong to be exorcized, but it's also too strong to resist when the male members of the family are twenty-one on Halloween. At a downtown synagogue he found the elderly caretaker there by himself. My son slaughtered him and sliced up his body in the way that only a medical student would know how to do.

"He made sure the murder would never be solved, but my son discovered that the caretaker was a Holocaust survivor with children and grandchildren. It wasn't bad enough that he had killed an innocent old man while enacting a centuries' old ritual of vengeance against his kind—he killed someone who had survived the most extensive acts of hatred ever against the Jewish people. My son was devastated when he learned this, and he determined that he would never marry or have children."

"That was another thing I wondered," I said, "why members of your family didn't just refuse to have children."

"Again, the dybbuk is too strong. My son made that promise to us all, but he didn't know that his girlfriend was already pregnant with twins. My grandson Barry is one of those twins. And now Barry's girlfriend wants to get married, and she's dying to have children. Although maybe that's not quite the right way to put it . . ."

"Do the women of the family know about this curse?"

"We always find out, Maurice. We always find out."

4

The Friedmans lived in a picture-perfect subdivision in Bloomfield Hills. Picture-perfect, that is, if you were an executive in one of the automobile companies. Or a top-flight surgeon, as Barry's father was. The sprawling three-story Tudor home had two Mercedes Benzes in the driveway and a half-acre of lawn in the front. The sun had gone down by then, and a Hunter's moon had risen, a full orange disk in the cloudless sky. Children out in their costumes filled the sidewalks, trooping from house to house with shopping bags stuffed with goodies, some bags larger than the children toting them. Parents accompanied their children carrying beverages in steaming mugs and lit the sidewalks with flashlights, though the moon was so bright it cast their shadows.

Just as Sarah said, Barry's parents were out on the front porch under their home's portico doling out Snickers and M&Ms to the trick-or-treaters. They both gave Sarah a hug and she asked, "Where are the kids?"

The parents shared a nervous look. They knew what tonight meant; they knew what was in store. Barry's father, especially, having gone through this already, understood. And they also understood they were powerless to stop it.

Sarah introduced me to them, Jack and Estelle. Barry's father Jack looked defeated, like someone caught in a trap set four hundred years ago.

"Our daughter Shari's with her boyfriend at a Halloween party. We don't know where Barry is," Barry's mother admitted. "He promised us—*promised* us—that he wouldn't give in to his"—here she threw an uncertain look at me—"his destiny tonight, but then he wouldn't tell us where he was going or what he was doing."

"We do know he's with his girlfriend," Jack said. He stared at me hard, as though memorizing my features.

His intense gaze discomfited me. "Have we met before?" I asked.

He shook his head and I asked, "Where does his girlfriend live?"

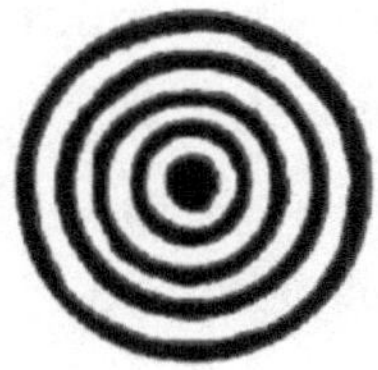

Barry's girlfriend, Shelley, lived in the same subdivision, several streets over. We drove carefully, avoiding the kids out in their costumes on this warm October night that was almost as bright as day.

At Shelley's house, only the mother was sitting on the porch handing out candy. She was an attractive woman with deep brown eyes; I thought if her daughter was as good-looking as the mother, she would be stunning indeed, a partner any man would be proud of. As a life-long loner, I had a pang of envy for that part of Barry's life—but only that one part.

"Do you know where the kids are?" Sarah asked.

I thought it would be too much to expect for her to say Shelley and Barry were in the back of the house, watching television.

And in fact, it was. She told Sarah, "They're out at Becker's Farm, putting on a Halloween play."

I could tell from the way Sarah reacted that this was not good news.

Shelley's mother continued: "I didn't know your son had raised such a dedicated genealogist."

Sarah was too distracted to wonder about that, but I said, "Sorry, what do you mean?"

"Barry has been asking me and my husband about our family trees. I asked him why, and he just said he was interested in history. So he's been compiling ours. He said he's going to surprise Shelley with it."

5

Sarah told me Becker's Farm was out in the country, north of the metropolitan area. I drove fast—more aware than ever that time was passing quickly on this Halloween night when Barry Friedman's most evil spirit would come out to wreak havoc.

It took three-quarters of an hour to get to the farm. On the way there, Sarah asked me how I got involved in paranormal investigations. I told her that I, like Barry, was interested in history, especially history that was out of the ordinary. As an investigator I was basically a researcher who delved into the history of so-called supernatural events to try to get to the bottom of hauntings, spirit possessions, and so on. My adoptive father was a history professor, and it seemed natural for me to follow in his footsteps, but with my own special twist.

The closer we got to our destination, the quieter Sarah became. She seemed to be turning inward, as if she were distraught by what she might find—and what we had to do—when we arrived. I tried to get her to tell me more about the family history of Ezra's dybbuk, but she was too distracted to say much. I think the enormity of what she had asked me to do was sinking in as the miles brought us closer to her grandson. I wondered if she was going to have the courage to let me go through with what she had hired me to do.

To be honest, I wondered if I did, too. I had done my share of engaging demons and ghosts and other paranormal beings as the needs arose, but never had I had the occasion to kill a human being, even one who harbored a spirit as deadly as Ezra's. Would I be able to go through with it? Usually, the process was to try to find the evil spirit, and only occasionally have to do battle with it. But I couldn't remember an instance where I had deliberately set out to kill the person whom the spirit had possessed. Tonight would be a new experience for me. I determined to do whatever I could to rid Barry of the dybbuk first without having to kill the young man.

Becker's Farm was an actual working farm, and was also attached to a corn maze, a cider mill, and a small amusement park for the kids. In addition, there were also hayrides, pony rides inside a corral, a park with games and bales of hay for children to clamber over, and wooden boards painted with pumpkins and witches and ghosts with holes for the kids (and parents, if they wanted) to stick their faces through and get their pictures taken.

At the center of it all were two large canvas tents. One seemed to be set up as a haunted house; I could hear unearthly moans and shrieks coming from it as kids and their parents went in one side and came out the other, laughing in fright. From the other tent I heard children's laughter and applause.

Sarah and I went into that one, hoping to find Barry's play. Sure enough, a troupe was putting on a skit on a raised platform at one end of the tent. A handful of men and women were dressed in Halloween costumes—the cast included Dracula, Frankenstein, the Bride of Frankenstein with a tall, Marge Simpson-like hairpiece, the Wolfman, a witch, and two actors dressed in lederhosen and drindl as Hansel and Gretel. It wasn't hard to grasp what was going on: the actors were doing a broad imitation of their monsters' movie images, trying to scare Hansel and Gretel in hopes of capturing them and popping them into a large prop oven so they could eat them. The kids for their part were outwitting the clumsy monsters at every turn, tricking them one-by-one into falling into the oven and comically perishing. At the end of the playlet, only Hansel and Gretel were left, holding two gigantic bags of candy. They passed out the candy to all the children in the tent audience, and at the curtain call all the monsters reassembled onstage and took their bows, still pretending to play their parts.

When the other actors went backstage, Dracula remained on the platform. He gazed around at the people remaining in the tent with a theatrical malevolent glower, and then swept his cloak across his eyes and rushed offstage.

"That was Barry," Sarah told me.

"Dracula?"

"Yes."

"He's got some good comedy chops."

"He does," Sarah said. "And the Bride of Frankenstein was played by his girlfriend, Shelley."

"They're a good comedy duo."

She couldn't answer. Now that we were here, she was starting to tremble, I assumed with fright at the enormity of what was to come. I put my hand on her arm and said, "Let's find Barry and talk to him, Sarah."

She couldn't answer. Was she changing her mind about this?

Our first order of business was getting hold of Barry, so I concentrated on that and tried not to think about what we would do when we found him. We went backstage in the theatre tent, which was really just an area set off from the front by a curtain. The actors had another show to perform in a half-hour, so they were lounging around in costume, drinking from an urn what smelled like warm spiced cider and munching on doughnuts from the cider mill. I also smelled the suspiciously skunky odor of cannabis.

Barry/Dracula wasn't back there. Nor was Shelley, the Bride of Frankenstein.

The Wolfman said they had both just slipped out the back of the tent. Sarah and I went looking for them.

We searched all over the farm but couldn't find them—they weren't in the cider mill, or the farm market, or any of the amusement and games areas. Finally, we decided to check the haunted house tent. Sarah must have had a premonition because she held my hand as we walked in; her own hand was ice cold.

As haunted houses go, it was pretty low-rent: lots of cheesy skeletons and mannequins dressed like farmers, fake bats dangling from the ceiling, Halloween-style cobwebs like the ones people put in their bushes every Halloween. The most disturbing part was the sound track of moans and groans and chains rattling. We both expected to see Barry at every turn in the trail leading through the haunted tent, but didn't see him or Shelley.

At the end of the path, a live actor jumped out from behind a pile of hay bales shouting, "BOOOO!" He made us both jump, but again it wasn't Barry Friedman.

And then we were out into the night air.

The sky was still clear; the Hunter's moon was still bright enough to cast shadows over the dark grounds. I was becoming more conscious of time passing... in a few hours, Halloween would be over, which meant that Barry would have to do his deed soon.

We saw the witch from the Halloween skit passing by and I asked her if she had seen either Barry or Shelley.

"I thought I just saw them headed for the cider mill. If you find them, could you remind them we're on again in ten minutes?"

"Will do," I replied.

Sarah grabbed my arm. "Wait," she said. "Let's go home. I can't go through with this."

"We're here. Let's at least talk to Barry and see if we can keep him from fulfilling his curse."

Sarah and I traipsed over to the cider mill, where, among the fragrant aromas of apples and frying donuts, we didn't see either Sarah's grandson or his girlfriend. It was coming up to nine o'clock, when Becker Farms shut down for the night. People were lined up at the cash registers to check out with their bushels of apples and jars of jelly and preserves.

"I'm getting worried," Sarah said, as though reading my mind. "It's getting late. Look, let's just go home."

"We're here, Sarah," I said again. "We might as well find Barry. We might be able to save someone's life tonight."

She looked like she wanted to tell me something, but she swallowed it and reluctantly agreed to stay.

Becker's Farm was starting to empty out as families went home. Sarah and I searched through the market section of the cider mill, as well as through the open kitchen where the apple presses were being cleaned and the vats were frying the last batches of donuts. Nothing.

We went around the outside of the cider mill to the rear. As we approached the pair of large trash dumpsters at the back of the building, we heard a woman's cry and then the "oof" of a body hitting the ground.

Sarah and I glanced at each other in horror. I tore around the corner of the building.

One small spotlight attached to the wall of the cider mill shone onto the two dumpsters, but the moon was so bright we didn't need it. Standing in between the bins, Barry Friedman in his long Dracula cape loomed over a pile of clothes on the ground.

"Barry," I called.

Barry looked up.

I have never seen a face as twisted in hatred as his was.

With a grisly smile, he showed me his blood-spattered face. In one hand was a large rock dark with blood.

I looked from him to the bundle of clothes on the ground and realized it was a body. The tall Marge Simpson wig was askew on her head but I knew the woman was Barry's girlfriend Shelley.

I knelt next to her to feel for a pulse. There was none. The side of her head was staved in. It looked like Barry had repeatedly bashed her head with the rock he still held. Her sightless eyes were fixed on Barry standing over her. I was right: in life she was as pretty as her mother. I didn't know her but I achingly grieved her death.

"Oh no!" Sarah gasped. "Barry, no—not Shelley!"

I stood. Barry was no longer the stage-caricature that he affected as an actor joking around in a Halloween skit. Now the look in his eye and the twisted grimace on his face were the very outward signs of evil.

Sarah began to cry. "Oh Barry, what have you done?"

"Fulfilled my destiny," he said in a deep, raspy, trance-like voice different from his broadly affected Transylvanian stage accent. This voice was not put on; it came from deep within him, and from deep within the chaotic history that he shared with his grandmother Sarah and the rest of his family going back generations to the Polish shtetl.

Sarah fell against the back wall of the cider mill. "Oh, but Shelley? Shelley!"

"I had to," Barry's trance-voice said. "Had to."

He looked down at Shelley's body, then back up at me. The fury in his eyes began to dissipate, and he seemed to be coming out of his trance. He looked at his grandmother, then back at Shelley on the ground as his eyes cleared and it dawned on him what he had just done. As I watched him, his expression dissolved into one of acute horror.

He looked down at the blood-covered rock and fell to his knees over Shelley's corpse, shouting, "Noooo!"

He began pounding his own head with the rock. I knelt beside him and tried to hold his arms before he did any damage.

But he was too fast and strong for me. Shouting an unearthly cry of despair, he twisted out of my grip. He dropped the rock and made a grab for the gun at my belt. He jerked it out of its holster, held it to his head, and without a moment's hesitation fired.

He toppled over sideways.

I leaned over him. Somehow he was still breathing despite the wound in the side of his head. I knew he would be dead by the time an ambulance arrived, so calling one would be futile. And in fact, while I watched, the life went out of his eyes as he died in front of me. After spending his life possessed by an evil spirit, he was now possessed by death.

Then something else happened.

At the moment of his death, a gray vapor rose from his body, a fog that swirled around as though caught in an eddy of air—the chill of it made me shiver—and then it drifted over me. It settled on me and sank through my clothes and into my body with a sound of electrical sparks snapping. A cold, damp presence enveloped me and froze me down to my bones.

I tried to think of something to do to keep this from happening, but I was powerless.

Sarah gasped and collapsed, clutching her heart.

She stopped breathing. I made myself move with stiff, icy arms and legs and began CPR on her. I pinched her nose and tried to breathe life back into her. The frozen fog that had settled into me made her lips feel scorching on my own.

I kept at it, but it was no use. She was gone.

But she got her wish—Ezra's ancient dybbuk had abandoned her grandson.

And entered me.

The state police had jurisdiction in that part of the county, so they came. EMTs came, too, but the three bodies on the ground behind the cider mill were past being revived.

I explained to the police as much as I thought I could share. I left out the part about Ezra's curse; the cops were suspicious enough of me already—standing there amid three dead bodies with blood on my hands—and I didn't feel like being locked up for insanity as well as murder. No, I told them that Barry murdered his fiancée in a moment of psychosis, and once he realized what he'd done, the shock of it made him grab my weapon and kill himself. His frail grandmother Sarah, witness to all this, perished from a heart attack no doubt brought on by the terrible scene that played out before her. I explained our presence there by saying Sarah wanted to see her grandson act in the Halloween playlet and I was a family friend, and we blundered into this tragedy.

The state cops took me down to the nearest station and sweated me overnight to try and break my story and get me to confess to three murders. I say "sweated," but in fact I was freezing. The new presence in my body seemed to lower my temperature by ten degrees. The cops asked me why I carried a gun; they were not happy to learn I was a private detective. I left out the paranormal part, which would have made them even more unhappy. They took my clothes for analysis, but found no blood spatter or gunpower residue. Ultimately, there was no forensic evidence linking me to any of the deaths. They had to let me go.

6

Barry and Shelley's family, being Jewish, sat shiva, the mourning ritual for their lost children. For Barry's parents, the occasion was doubly sad because they were also mourning Sarah Friedman, the matriarch of the family.

At Shelley's house, I met her father, Ben, and offered my condolences. I'd never seen a grown man cry the way he cried.

I realized I never knew Shelley's last name. When he'd gotten the tears out of his system for the time being, he introduced himself as Ben Simpson.

"I know," he said, "that's an odd name for a Jew. My grandfather changed it when he came through Ellis Island in the early nineteen-hundreds."

"Lots of immigrants' names were changed back then."

"I guess he wanted something less ethnic.The family's original name in Europe was Silberberg."

Silberberg.

The name stopped me. I thought back to the story that Sarah told me in my office, the tale about the two best friends in Poland who had made a pact for their children to wed. Except one of them had gone back on his promise, and as a result Leah Silberberg never married her true love, Ezra Rosenthal. It was that betrayal of the word given to a friend that had begun four hundred years of spiritual possession and violence that traveled across an ocean of time and space to bring a different pair of lovers together.

And ultimately to separate them both by death.

Now I understood Barry's interest in genealogy… he was tracing the spirit's lineage back to Shelley's family in Poland. And to her great-great-great-great ancestor, Shmuel Silberberg.

And now that same spirit with Ezra's curse possessed me. But wait—hadn't Sarah said the dybbuk only possessed Ezra's male descendants? How was that possible?

There could only be one answer.

At the Friedmans' house, the mirrors were covered and the cushions had been removed from all the sofas and chairs, as the shiva ritual required. I found Barry's father Jack by himself, sitting in a room in the back of the house.

"Remember me?" I asked.

"Of course."

"Please accept my condolences on your losses."

"Thank you," Jack said. We shook hands. "This used to be Barry's room," he said. He gazed around at the remnants of a boy's life that had been extinguished forever—posters of the

Rolling Stones, a baseball bat and glove, a pair of ice skates draped over the back of the desk chair and a hockey stick leaning in a corner, a trio of trophies on a shelf.

Jack gave me the same look he had the other day, a deep, searching gaze. "It has you now, doesn't it?" he asked.

"Yes."

"I can tell."

"Your mother told me the spirit only possesses members of the male line of the family."

"Yes. And now it's got you."

"Which means I'm part of your family."

"You are. Sarah never said anything about it?"

"No. She may have meant to, but... well, things didn't work out that way. What more can you tell me?"

"You know the first part of it," Jack said. "She and my father had two children, twins, me and my sister, as our entire line did. But there was also a third child, born later."

"Me."

He nodded. "Knowing what happened with male children in our family, Sarah couldn't bear the thought of bringing another boy into our cursed history. So they put you up for adoption right after you were born."

"And made up the false story about my mother dying giving birth to me."

"Yes. When my wife and I had Barry and her sister, Sarah and my father agonized over what to do about the dybbuk's curse. Exorcisms never worked, so she finally thought she would try something else. Perhaps an unaffected male member of the bloodline could end the dybbuk's reign in our family."

"By killing Barry and ending the spirit that way?" This was what Sarah had come to my office asking me to do.

"No. She thought a male member of the bloodline unconnected with the family might attract the dybbuk away from Barry and leave his curse unfulfilled."

"She wanted the dybbuk to leave her grandson alone and attach itself to me?"

"I thought it was a terrible, foolish idea, and I told her so. But she was desperate to save her grandson from the curse."

"So she tracked me down, and discovered, conveniently, I was a paranormal investigator."

"Yes. She thought that increased the odds that you might know how to deal with the dybbuk. I'm sorry," he added. "That was a horrible thing to do to you, using you as bait."

"More like a scapegoat, attracting the evil away from your son."

"Yes," he admitted. "I suppose."

"It's small consolation for either of us, but toward the end she regretted it and tried to get me to back off. But by then, events were already in process."

He said nothing.

"I guess this means we're brothers," I said.

He didn't reply to that, either.

There was nothing more to say.

7

I never went back to the Friedman home. I never saw my new-found brother again. I tried to reenter my life and go about the business of paranormal investigations, but it was hard to move forward from the Halloween night when I discovered a past I never knew I had, and gained a future I could never imagine.

Ever since then, I have felt it lurking inside me, always there, morning to night, a cold gobbet of evil centered in the pit of my stomach but spreading, numbingly cold, throughout the rest of my body.

And what could I do to fight against it—against this spirit that had defied generations of rabbis and attempts to purge it from its hosts? There was nothing I could do, no paranormal investigator like myself whom I could consult, nothing that could undo what could not be undone over four centuries.

No, it worked within me the same way it worked in Barry Friedman, his father, and every male going back to Ezra Rosenthal. I was over twenty-one, but not immune to the dybbuk's curse. As every Halloween approached, the evil spirit took over my life as it had controlled the lives of generations of Rosenthal men and boys, directing me to commit the vilest, bloodiest acts against my will. I've tried to end my life to end the terror this demon exacts on the world… but even then, the dybbuk prevents me from going through with it. It doesn't just live inside me; it has *become* me.

Even so, I've mustered the strength to keep myself from passing on the dybbuk to the children I will never have; a vasectomy ended that possibility. Still, I'm the prisoner of a long, lonely life of waiting for the months to pass each year until the evil spirit shows itself again, unbidden and unwanted, and makes me a conduit for its gory vengeance on another terrible night in late October.

FINN'S FRIEND

Andrew Charles Lark

And these children that you spit on
As they try to change their worlds
Are immune to your consultations
They're quite aware of what they're going through.
—David Bowie, "Changes"

1

Logan spun around and gazed into the floor length mirror. "YESTH!" he shouted, super satisfied at what he saw. "This is the besth Count Dracula costume ever!" The brocade smoking jacket, the crisply starched white shirt, the red sash, and black pleated slacks all fit perfectly. He especially liked how Mom slicked his thick, unruly dark hair back with some smelly, gooey gel from her make-up drawer, and the shiny result far outweighed the stink of it. The crowning touch, however, was the set of sharp, mechanical fangs that grew longer when he pressed his tongue on a lever hidden behind his two front teeth. Mom had found them on Amazon.

"Brandon and Brice are gonna be thsoooo jealous!" he lisped, as he pushed on the hidden lever, watching the sharp fangs grow long then retract. He especially loved how the fangs clicked. "Oh my God! YESTH!" They were totally worth whatever she paid for them.

Mom stood just behind Logan, admiring her creation. It was moments like this that made working two jobs worth the exhaustion—almost. If only Logan were capable of showing even a scintilla of compassion, and it didn't help that he had lately befriended the two biggest bullies in the neighborhood—Brandon and Brice—otherwise known as the terrible twins.

Mom flicked a curly lock of blonde hair from her eyes, then moved in to make one final adjustment to his collar. "Logan, I didn't make your costume to make your friends jealous, I hope you know."

"Whatever." said Logan, knocking her hand away. His black, patent-leather shoes tapped out an impatient cadence. "Now, help me with my cape. I don't wanna be late."

"Don't bark orders at me, young man! Remember who's boss around here!" Mom had been doing her very best, but in addition to working two jobs, she and Logan were dealing with having lost Logan's father in a military training accident five years prior, and her concerns over Logan's attitude were borderline overwhelming, and she was at a loss over how to deal with his many behavioral issues that had been cropping up lately. She decided to use the one ace she had up her sleeve for tonight and threw caution to the wind to see if it would help put an end to Logan's aggressiveness, or at least move his needle in a more compassionate direction.

"Oh, I almost forgot," she said, tying the cape around his neck, "you boys are going to have one more trick-or-treat friend tonight." Logan already knew what she was going to say—the twins had texted him earlier while he was walking home from school, and they'd used the intervening time to hatch a plan.

"Oh? Who?" said Logan dripping with feigned interest.

"You know that new kid? Finn?"

"Hmm… Finn? Oh, yesth, Finn," he replied, playing with his teeth in the mirror.

"It would mean the world to me if you and the twins took him along tonight."

"Of course, Mom. You've worked so hard on my costume, it's the least I can do." Mom looked down skeptically at her fourteen-year-old.

"Are you being for real? I never know with you sometimes."

"You know he's home-schooled, right?"

"I'd heard that," said Mom.

"So I think it's kinda hard for him to make friends. But he does have an imaginary friend," said Logan, snickering.

"How do you know that?"

"Kevin told me. He sees Finn in the park at night sometimes, talking and playing with someone who's not there."

"Well, that's just sad, but that probably means he's lonely and could use a real friend. Don't you think?"

"Oh, we're gonna be his friends tonight."

"Well, it'd be very sweet of you boys, and I think you'd make his night."

"He's going to have quite the night, I promise."

"Do you mean it? Really?" said Mom, her skepticism lingering.

"Oh, I really, REALLY mean it!" he said, baring his fangs in a malevolent smile. He lifted his webbed cape high, then watched it billow gently downward, enveloping him shoulder to knees.

"Then why are you smiling like that?" she asked. "I mean it, if anything happens to him—"

"Jesus, Mom, give me a break!"

"Don't talk to me that way! And I swear if you're lying this will be the last time you'll ever go trick-or-treating!" she said.

"I'm fourteen, and this'll prolly be my last time anyway, so... don't wait up!" Then, with an artful twirl, Logan grabbed his matching black trick-or-treat bag and fled out the door and into the night, his black, webbed cape flapping an *adieu*.

"Be careful," she shouted as Logan disappeared around the hedgerow toward Brandon and Brice's... but she quickly forgot all about him when she noticed an adorable little girl in a bumblebee costume clumsily ascend the porch, her father, a pace behind, minding her steps, but then something strange dashed around them and into her house—*a shadow?* she thought, *or maybe a trick of light? Strange...* "Twick-awe-tweet," said the bumblebee, holding her plastic pumpkin aloft.

"Aww, what a darling little bumblebee! Here you are, sweetie," she said, thinking, *how nice it would have been to give birth to a girl instead of a boy.*

2

Logan sprang onto the twin's porch and skipped toward the door, passing a bunch of tied corn stalks and an anorexic scarecrow sitting in a lawn chair, its burlap head bowed as if ashamed of its scrawny physique. Tufts of straw poked through the rips of its patchwork hobo outfit, and a black felt hat capped its head. Three grim jack-o-lanterns flickered at its feet, and it was so dark already, *Too dark,* thought Logan as he reached for the doorbell. The scarecrow's burlap head jerked up and looked at Logan with coal-black eyes.

"Holy Crap!!!" shouted Logan jumping back, startled.

"Sorry. I didn't mean to scare you," said the scarecrow, unfolding itself out of the chair, now standing and staring at Logan, its head cocked oddly. Logan realized that the scarecrow was Finn, and his flash of fear morphed to annoyance.

"You didn't scare me, dork! And what're you doin' just sittin' there like some kinda freak?" Finn's burlap head bowed in shame.

"Sorry. I tried the doorbell, but no one answered, so—"

"Well jus' so you know, we don't wanna go trick-or-treating with you, but we're being forced to, so—"

"Sorry but, you guys don't hafta take me," said Finn.

"Oh no! You're coming! And stop saying sorry every five seconds. It's annoying."

"Sorry."

"Pshh… you're hopeless," said Logan, rolling his eyes, and even though Finn's scarecrow costume freaked him out a little, he'd never admit to it. Besides, it didn't really matter, because Logan and the twins had plans for Finn, and he'd never want to go trick-or-treating again after they'd finished with him. Then without warning, the sugar maple that canopied over the lawn yawed out a loud creak, shook violently, and a large branch crashed hard onto the bed of mulch surrounding its trunk.

"Woah!" said Logan. "Didja see that?"

Finn just smiled a knowing smile.

Logan jumped down onto the lawn and ran toward the fallen branch then looked up into the canopy, and in spite of the dark, he swore he saw… something. *What is that?* he thought, as whatever it was slinked behind a high-up tangle of black. Just then Brandon and Brice bashed through the front door in a clumsy jumble of chubby arms, legs, and pear-shaped torsos. They were dressed in dark blue suits, white shirts, and red neckties that dangled way down past their crotches. Atop each of their heads sat orangey-blonde wigs that reminded Logan of the cotton candy at the fair that he puked-up on the double Ferris wheel last summer, and the memory brought on by those cheap wigs almost made him wretch. Red MAGA caps atop those ugly wigs left no doubt that Brandon and Brice were out to make Halloween great again.

Logan turned and would have sworn on a stack of Bibles that he saw something slip into their house. It was weird—a dark sparkle... or something, but it happened so quickly, if he had blinked he would have missed it. He looked back up into the canopy of the tree and whatever it was he saw up there had vanished. *I must be seeing things,* he thought.

"And behave yourselves!" shouted the twin's mom through the chaos. "I don't want any phone calls!"

"Ah suck it, bitch!" yelled Brice over his shoulder as the screen door slapped shut. He noticed Logan in his Count Dracula costume, balanced on the fallen branch, looking up into the canopy of their tree.

"What happened to our tree?" said Brandon.

"I dunno, it was so weird," said Logan. "We were jus' standing here and all the sudden this branch came crashing down."

"When my dad gets back from bowling, he's gonna be pissed," said Brice, standing on the driveway, his hands on his hips surveying the damage, then he looked over at Finn, now standing off in the shade of the wounded tree. "Ooooh, a scarecrow!" he said. "Izzat Finn?"

"Yeah. I'm Finn," he replied, walking toward Brice, offering his hand. "Hi." The gesture was ignored.

"So we're trick-or-treating with a scarecrow and Count Fagula?" said Brandon, standing on the sidewalk.

"Fuckin' lame!"

"Yeah? Well check these out," said Logan. He jumped off the fallen branch, flashed his fangs up then down, and hoisted his webbed cape aloft. "Thsee these fangs? I'll suck the blood out your neck holes!"

"Yeah? How 'bout suck on this instead!" said Brice, grabbing his junk and shaking it. "Haw-haw!"

"Come on, dickwads!" shouted Brandon, already halfway across the tree-lined street. "Let's make Halloween great again!"

"Yeah! Let's do this," replied Brice. "Come on, scarecrow, or Finn, or whatever. This'll be one Halloween you'll never forget!"

Finn took one last look at the fallen branch, then peered up into the tree and smiled. It didn't happen very often, but when his Friend did things like this, it made him happy. It gave him confidence. Initially, the prospect of going trick-or-treating with these boys made him uneasy. Even though Finn possessed great powers, being the bait was always nerve-wracking, and he knew viciousness when he saw it, and the twins were vicious to their core. Stupid too. That was obvious. Logan, the boy dressed as Count Dracula, didn't seem as bad. Sure, he was a prick, but there was something about him that seemed redeemable. He'd take a wait-and-see attitude on Logan. But the branch falling down was an omen. He knew that no matter what happened, he'd be safe, and that his Friend would protect him, even from afar. This was going to be quite a night.

"You guys coming or what?" shouted Brandon, already across the street. "I ain't got time for no slowpokes."

"Hold your horses, bro. We're coming," said Logan, ten paces behind and catching up quickly, his black cape fluttering. Brice and Finn followed a few houses behind when Brice put his arm around Finn's scrawny shoulder and leaned into his burlap covered ear. Finn felt something splat onto the bottom of his candy bucket.

"I got a question for you, Mr. Scarecrow," said Brice. "You bringin' your imaginary friend with you tonight? Yeah, I heard about him, so don't play stupid." Finn winced at Brice's heinous breath, then he turned and looked at him, his black eyes flashing anger through ragged burlap eyeholes.

"None of your business," said Finn. He wriggled out of Brice's embrace then quick-timed his pace to get away from the stench.

"Trick-or-treat! Trick-or-treat!" shouted Brice, a few steps behind. "There's a surprise in your bucket, freak! Haw-haw!" Finn walked under the glow of a streetlight, looked down, and saw a big, smelly dog turd steaming in the bottom of his candy bucket. Incensed, he turned around and whipped the bucket at Brice, which hit him square in the chest. The turd dislodged and thwacked onto Brice's white shirt then splattered all over his black dress shoes. Brice dropped his candy bag and looked down at the smelly mess, then he looked up at Finn, his blotchy, adolescent face red and pocked with rage.

"You skinny, little fuck! You're so dead." Finn stood his ground and looked at Brice; his head tilted slightly, the brim of his scarecrow hat cast a black shadow across his face, and although he was stick-thin, he did have some height to him — an inch on the twins, and two inches on Logan, at least.

"If you wouldn't have dropped that deuce into my bucket, then you wouldn't be wearing it now, would you?" said Finn, emboldened by his Friend's destruction of the tree branch a few minutes prior. By now a few of the other neighborhood trick-or-treaters had gathered and formed a circle around Brice and Finn. They all recognized Brice through his Trump costume, and a few murmurs rose up: "That kid's so dead," and "He better haul ass if he wants to live," and "Brice is gonna kill the new kid."

3

Logan and Brandon had made the corner and turned left at Birkhill Street, already walking up to their third front door. "Hey, we're way ahead of 'em. Shouldn't we wait?" asked Logan, spinning to make his cape billow. He loved billowing his cape.

"I said I ain't slowin' down for no slowpokes," said Brandon. "So screw 'em."

"What about our plan?" asked Logan. "What about beatin' the shit outta—"

"I tole my dumb-ass brother that if we get separated, to just meet at the park. I'll text him when we get there."

"Well, I hope your dumb-ass brother doesn't screw up," said Logan, then, for no reason at all, Brandon shoved Logan hard, and he went flying into a hedge of boxwoods that lined the walk toward Mr. Marsh's front door.

"Don't call my dumb-ass brother, dumb-ass!" Brandon said, pointing at Logan as he untangled himself from the hedge. Brandon laughed at his own hilarity. Logan brushed a few branches off his costume, looking very irritated and hoping that nothing snagged the satin brocade.

"Hey you kids! What'd you do to my bush?" said Mr. Marsh, framed in his doorway and dressed as a psycho clown, and there was certainly something psycho about the vibe he was giving off.

Mr. Marsh had been diagnosed with an inoperable brain tumor four months prior, and the doctors let him know that his condition was terminal, but instead of crawling into a shell of despair and self-pity, he decided to embrace what time he had left and to live with an unbridled enthusiasm. He was enjoying this year's parade of trick-or-treaters ascending his porch, but then something odd happened. At first he thought it was simply a trick of light, or those weird crescents of twinkling colors that would occasionally manifest in his vision as he went about his day, but this was different. A thin slip of a shadow crept up onto his porch, almost imperceptibly, but Mr. Marsh did see it. It flashed by, past him, then curved back and slammed into him in a shiver and shock of cold that left him light-headed and off balance. *What's happening to me?* he thought. *Is this the onset of a new symptom?* His fears were palpable, but he was doing his best to shove them back... at least until the last piece of candy was picked from the large bowl on his porch. He looked down at the chubby kid dressed as Trump, and again asked,

"What'd you do to my bushes?"

"It's trick-or-treat, ain't it?" said Brandon, laughing. *This clown dude was definitely drunk or high on something,* thought Brandon.

"Huh? What about it?" Mr. Marsh replied, trying to shake off this sudden fog. He opened his screen door then barged down the stoop, the screen door slapping shut behind him. Logan skittered out of the way as Mr. Marsh barreled by, off-balance in his ridiculous polka dot pantaloons, toward the damage.

"You don't treat? We trick!" said Brandon. Mr. Marsh bent down to inspect the damage but fell to his knees..

"Well... I, I got candy right over there in that—" said Mr. Marsh, pointing toward the big bowl on the porch, but his words wouldn't come out because it felt like his brain had been clotted by cataracts. He looked back at his seriously crushed boxwoods. "You little shits!" he roared, attempting to get back onto his feet. "Where do you live? Your parents are gonna pay for this! Hey! Where you goin? Get back here," he shouted at Logan and Brandon as they high-tailed it off into the dim orange and black glow of Birkhill Street, zigzagging through the maze of trick-or-treaters.

Mr. Marsh shifted onto all fours and with great effort, managed to get back on to his feet. He looked off in the direction of where the two boys had fled, then looked down at his damaged hedgerow. He threw his hands up, disgusted, then trudged unsteadily toward the door. He passed by the big bowl of candy, and when he got inside he snapped the porch light off.

What's happening to me, he thought, ripping the clown mask off his head and tossing it onto the vestibule bench next to the framed, full-length mirror that leaned against the wall. But when he caught a glimpse of his reflection, what he saw didn't make any sense. He stumbled toward the mirror bewildered and confused, but the confusion quickly ascended to abject terror as he moved in closer and touched the thing his face had become – a melting and bubbling goo of flesh. He shrieked and a fountain of phlegm, clotted chunks, and bloody offal spewed from his mouth and ran down the mirror as a split formed at the top of his sagging brow, causing his eyeballs to drop from their sockets. They now dangled by their optic nerves. He clutched his chest and felt a mortal pang reverberate down his left arm and wrist. He collapsed hard onto the floor and watched as that thing, that something, that strange slip of a shadow, whatever it was... leave him.

Now everything was normal—his thoughts, his sight, his equilibrium and clarity... even his face. But it took him a second or two to realize that he was looking down upon his corpse lying prone on the floor.

He saw the shadow figure clearly as it moved in toward his corpse, shimmering in its blackness, like a sparkly, paper cut-out of a human figure. It crouched and tenderly caressed Mr. Marsh's cheek, then its hand dove through the skin, the skull, and deeper still, feeling and probing through the folds and contours of gray matter. It found what it was looking for and pulled it from Mr. Marsh's skull, leaving not a trace of its cranial intrusion. It ascended from its crouch and stood next to the corpse, tall and wisp-thin.

Mr. Marsh looked at the shadow figure, then looked down at his own face, which stared blankly at the ceiling, the back of his head plastered to the vestibule floor—eyes bulging terror wide, and shoots of hair, stiff and shockingly white. This was such a strange perspective, *very surreal,* he thought. And there he hovered above his corpse for a bit.

The shadow figure's head snapped around and looked directly at Mr. Marsh's essence hovering above his body. It swiftly inhaled through multiple holes in its sparkly head and sucked the hovering essence into its shiny blackness. The shadow then cupped its hands, blew into them, and a brightly glowing orb ascended from out of its palms. The orb hovered until the shadow pointed at Mr. Marsh's corpse and the orb slowly descended and landed on Mr. Marsh's forehead. It rested there for a few seconds before absorbing deep into his skull. Mr. Marsh's body spasmed and jerked, then almost violently, he sucked air into his lungs with every ounce of strength his diaphragm could muster.

A few days later, Mr. Marsh's doctors would not be able to explain to him how or why his inoperable brain tumor had disappeared... this simply does not happen.

"We're way ahead of 'em now," said Logan, slowing to a walk. "Fer real, shouldn't we wait?" They were a block and a half ahead of Brice and Finn, at least, nearing the corner of Birkhill and Minden.

"No!" said Brandon, from behind, catching up, huffing and puffing. "I ain't got shit... for candy... and I wanna... load up... you wanna bail... go ahead... I don't... give a fuck."

"You're cold-hearted, bro. You know that? And why'd you push me back there?"

"I was just havin' fun... why you gettin' so triggered?" said Brandon.

"Whatever, dude. You almost ruined my costume."

"Whatsamatter, Count Fagula? Worried about your fancy costume?"

"It's better than your lame-ass Trump costume! And why you and Brice gotta dress the same? Talk about..." Out of nowhere, Brandon balled his fist, swung, and belted Logan square in the jaw. Logan's retractable fangs flew from his mouth and exploded into pieces when they struck the curb. Blood pooled up inside Logan's cheek where the fangs sliced into his flesh. He spit a gob of blood onto the pavement.

"You asshole! Look what you did! I'm bleeding! And my fangs!"

"Keep talkin' yer shit and I'll bust more than your fangs!" Logan looked Brandon up and down and decided right there and then that this dumb ass was no longer worth the time of day, and that as far as he was concerned, they were finished.

"You're a frickin' psycho, you know that? And your dumb-ass brother ain't any better. I'm done with both of you!" Once again, Brandon balled up his fist and swung hard, but this time Logan dodged out of reach, then took off left down Minden Street.

"I told you, keep talkin' yer shit and I'm gonna fuck you up!" yelled Brandon watching Logan disappear into the Halloween fray. *Fine. He was a pussy anyway, who needs him,* thought Brandon, still a little winded. Then he asked himself a serious question:

How can I make Halloween great again? I know! I'll get dad's golf cart! I'm tired of walkin' anyway. Then a sneer rippled across his pudgy cheeks as an idea slowly formed. *I'm gonna steal me some candy.*

4

The fight kept playing out in Brice's mind over and over, and how Finn was actually getting the best of him... at first. He felt the swelling and wondered if he'd have a black eye. He'd never hear the end of how the skinny new kid—who was totally psycho, with an imaginary friend—gave him a black eye! And another thing that really pissed Brice off was how the other trick-or-treaters were actually cheering for Finn! *That's some serious bullshit*, he thought. *They're lucky I didn't recognize them. I'll find out though, and they'll be sorry. Goddamn, will they be sorry!*

The fight turned when Brice got dirty and kicked Finn square in the balls, and that put a stop to him and his fan club. After that it was easy - he broke out a can of whoop-ass, jumped on top, and commenced with a beat down, pummeling Finn's head and face until some asshole going around with his two little kids pulled him off. Once free, Finn rushed off down Birkhill toward the park, but what bothered Brice most was how Finn laughed as he ran off, like the skinny little pussy he was. Finn's laugh got into Brice's head big time! *Nobody laughs at me,* he thought. "I ain't done with you, fucker!" yelled Brice.

"Watch your language, you bully," said the guy with the kids.

"Go fuck yourself, pedo!" yelled Brice, his middle-finger aloft as he broke into a half-jog toward home to change out of his shit-smeared costume. The man watched Brice cross the street wearing his dark blue suit, white shirt, and red necktie that dangled way down past his belly, that wig, and red MAGA cap and thought, *Wow! What an appropriate costume!* He took his crying kids by their hands.

"Hey guys. Let's go home and look through your candy, okay?" It was getting late anyway.

"Okay, Daddy," they replied, through sniffles.

On his way back home to change, Brice saw a couple of kids dressed like skeletons in fancy sequined clothes and sombreros walking toward him. Their costumes reminded him of some stupid cartoon about a Mexican boy who wanted to play the guitar, but his dead skeleton relatives tried to stop him, and it suddenly dawned on him that these skeleton kids were illegals from Mexico, stealing candy from American trick-or-treaters.

"Go back to Mexico!" shouted Brice as he passed them.

"Eat another Big Mac, Trump," said one of the skeletons, laughing.

If I wasn't covered in shit, I'd beat their asses, thought Brice. *Why are all these assholes laughing at me tonight?*

He arrived back home, stopped, and couldn't believe what he saw. He stood there on the driveway and looked up at the sugar maple. It had been stripped of all of its branches, and they'd been arranged in a spiral that circled the trunk.

"What the hell happened to our tree?" he said, walking around it. The bark had been stripped too, so all that was left was a tall, bare stalk, like a witch's finger pointing out the moon, betraying its hiding spot behind the swift, jagged clouds above.

"I'm home!" yelled Brice. "And didja see outside? What happened to our tree?" Brice hadn't noticed the strange shadow that had slipped into their home earlier as he and his twin had barged out of the front door to trick-or-treat with Logan and Finn. The shadow had found Brice's mom watching *Wheel of Fortune* in her bedroom. It charmed and put her into a deep sleep, and later, when Brice's father would get home, he would be charmed as well, and wouldn't notice that his prized sugar maple had been completely denuded of its branches that lay in a spiral on his lawn. He'd simply pull into his driveway, oblivious to the damage.

It didn't bother Brice that his mom hadn't replied, and that it was actually a good thing because now he wouldn't have to put up with any of her shit. *Mom's prolly in her room in one of her moods, with the TV at full blast as usual.*

"Is Dad still bowling? Wait till he sees what happened to our tree!" he shouted, bounding up the steps two at a time. He bee-lined into his bedroom where he rifled through a pile of dirty clothes in the corner.

"This'll do," he said, picking a white, ketchup-stained shirt out of the pile. *It's dark out. No one'll notice.* He kicked his shoes off and they dented the wall, leaving a shitty black scuff.

"My bad!" he yelled. He found his black tennis shoes, slipped them on, dashed out of his room, down the hall, to the stairs, then he abruptly stopped in front of his father's office door. *Should I?* he thought. *Fuck yeah! Why not? Just to scare 'em.* He quietly snuck in, walked behind his father's desk, crouched, and lifted the loose floorboard where his father hid his .32 caliber Glock, but it was gone.

Dammit, he thought. *Dad must've found a new hiding spot.*

"Smell you later!" he shouted, barging out of the house and into the night. Brice saw Brandon up ahead walking toward him alone. "Hey! What're you doing? Where's Logan at?"

"And where's Finn? You lose him already, dumbass?"

"No! He threw a pile of dog shit at me so I beat his ass. Where's Logan?"

"He got smart with me, so I punched him in the face and he ran off like a little bitch."

"Well this sucks. The night's ruined, and I don't hardly got any candy. What'll we do now?" asked Brice.

"I dunno about you, but I'm gettin' Dad's golf cart."

"Fuck yeah! I'm drivin'!" said Brice.

"The fuck you are, it was my idea! I'm drivin'!"

"I get to drive on the way back, then."

"We'll see. And what the fuck happened to our tree?" said Brandon.

5

Logan was embarrassed and sad to find himself trick-or-treating alone, but it was a lot better than going around with a bully who shoved and punched him. And he was really upset about the fangs Mom had bought him. He probed the deep gash inside his cheek with his tongue and it was still bleeding. He spit and sure enough, the gob was totally bloody. *God, I hope I don't need stitches,* he thought. *That's gonna suck if I do! Mom wasn't too thrilled about me bein' friends with them,* he thought. *I can tell. And she was right—Brandon and Brice are garbage, although she'd never say that. And I don't know what their problem is. They're totally rich but only want more and more, and boy, do they get whatever they want! But it's never enough with those two. They're mean and only care about themselves. Fuck them,* he thought. His mood lifted a little when he saw a couple kids costumed in beautifully detailed *Dia de los Muertos* costumes up ahead, walking toward him.

"Hey! Cool costumes, *amigos!*" said Logan as they passed.

"Thanks, Count! Yours too!" replied the taller one.

And then Logan thought about Finn. *You know, there's no reason in the world to be mean to someone just because they're new, and you were being a total dick to him earlier. And you gotta admit it, Logan, Finn's costume is pretty frickin' cool. It sure freaked you out when you first saw it! Yeah, he might be a little weird, but you're a little weird too, let's face it. And mom does so much for you, and you've been nothing but a jerk to her.* Logan stopped walking and looked up at the dark sky as tears pooled and trailed vertically down his temples. He was really depressed now and didn't feel like trick-or-treating anymore.

"Screw this. I'm going home," he said aloud. He peered into his black Halloween bag, the one Mom had sewn for him, thank you very much, and it only made him even more depressed. *Just looking at this candy is making me sick,* he thought. *I don't even want it anymore.* He turned around and sprinted up to the *Dia de los Muertos* boys.

"Hey guys?" said Logan.

"Oh! Hey! Count Dracula, what's up?"

"I, uh... just remembered, I'm not supposed to eat sweets anymore," he lied. "Because I'm... uh, dyslectic. That's what the doctor said. So I was wondering, would you like my candy?"

"Hey, that's really nice, but we can't take your candy!" said the taller of the boys.

"Speak for yourself, I'll take your candy, Count!" the shorter kid interjected, opening his sack and holding it out for Logan.

"You can have it. Here," said Logan, turning his bag upside down and dumping its contents into the shorter boy's sack.

"Thanks, man! That's so cool of you."

"Well, doctor's orders... you know?"

"Yeah, well I hope you get better, bro!" said the taller kid. He put his hand on Logan's shoulder.

"Me too. Get better," said the one who got the candy.

"Thanks, guys. Have a good one."

Logan climbed his porch steps and twisted the doorknob, but it was locked. *That's weird,* he thought. *Mom must've run out of candy already.* He knocked and rang the doorbell.

"I'm home," he said. "Mom! The door's locked, can you let me in?" He heard footsteps coming toward the door, but they sounded heavier than normal. The door opened and it was some guy he'd never seen before. A little girl in a bumblebee costume came up behind him and wrapped her arm around the man's leg. Her lips were smeared with chocolate.

"Sorry buddy, but we're all out of candy," said the man. Logan blanched. "Great costume though!"

"Uh... excuse me, but I live here! Where's my mom?" said Logan, surprised and perturbed. Then he heard mom's voice emanating from the kitchen.

"Is that another trick-or-treater? Tell 'em we're out of candy."

"Uh, no! It's some kid who says he lives here. Is this a joke? Are you tricking instead of treating?

"Hey mom!? Can you tell this guy to let me IN MY OWN HOUSE?" Mom appeared around the corner wearing an apron. Pregnant... like, the baby's gonna pop out at any minute, pregnant!

"Can I help you, young man? Are you lost? Do you need to call someone?" asked Mom. Logan's heart leapt into his throat throwing him backward, almost off the porch.

"Wait! Is this some kind of joke? This is my house! You're my mom! What the actual fuck is going on here!?" shouted Logan. Now Mom was angry. She cocked her chin, pointed at Logan, and let him have it.

"Okay, first off, I do not appreciate your language in the presence of my daughter, and secondly, if this is some sort of prank, it's not funny! So turn around and get walking. Now!" Logan stumbled backward over the iron railing and fell hard onto the grass. He got up and looked desperately at his very pregnant mom.

"This doesn't make any sense! What's happening? MOM! IT'S ME! LOGAN! I'M LOGAN! YOUR SON!" Now the man stepped out onto the porch holding his cellphone aloft, but Mom already had her cellphone to her ear and was talking into it.

"Buddy, I'm giving you five seconds to get off our property, or I'm calling the police. Have I made myself clear? This isn't funny anymore. Now go on, beat it!" Logan absolutely lost it and snapped.

"MOM, I'M REALLY SORRY ABOUT THE FANGS, BUT BRANDON PUNCHED ME AND I'M BLEEDING AND THEY BROKE AND I'M SORRY, I'M SO, SO, SORRY! FOR EVERYTHING!"

Now Mom came out onto the porch, planted her feet and crossed her arms.

"Young man, I don't know what your problem is, but you're obviously troubled. Now, I've already called the police, and I suggest you stick around and allow them to help you out... but it's your choice."

But for Logan there was no choice because nothing made sense anymore. His eyes shifted from his mom, to the man, then to the picture window where the little girl in the bumblebee costume stood looking at him. She bit into a piece of Halloween candy and her chocolate smeared lips broke into a big Cheshire smile... and then she waved buh-bye. The front door slammed shut and the porch light snapped off leaving him alone in the dark. Logan turned and bolted off, his cape flapping a second *adieu*.

6

"Where we goin'?" asked Brice. He was still stewing that he couldn't drive, but taking the golf cart was Brandon's idea. *Still,* he thought, *this is some serious bullshit. He always gets to drive!* Brice knew he'd get his turn behind the wheel though, even if it meant breaking out another can of whoop-ass. They sped down the driveway and over the sidewalk, scattering trick-or-treaters. "Outta the way, losers," shouted Brandon, blaring the horn.

"Shouldda just hit 'em," said Brice.

"Just you wait," said Brandon.

As they tore ass down the street, the golf cart could have easily been mistaken for a parade float, with a giant MAGA flag flapping above the right fender, and a giant Trump flag waving above the left fender. Slogans and political candidate stickers festooned every square inch of the expensive, streamlined, top of the line golf cart, while the twins rode high, costumed in glorious emulation of their president, their faces defiantly determined.

"I ain't got shit for candy because that Logan pussy was such a slowpoke, so the plan is to steal us some, got it? said Brandon.

"How?" asked Brice.

"I gotta explain everything? When I see someone... forget it. Just watch and learn from the master," said Brandon.

"Oh! I saw some Mexicans earlier when I was walking home, stealing candy from American trick-or-treaters," said Brice.

"Where?"

"On Birkhill. They were both wearing those big, stupid hats—"

"Sombreros?" said Brandon.

"Whatever. All I know is they were prolly illegals," said Brice.

"We'll keep an eye out for 'em." They sped up to the corner and turned right on Minden. Halfway down the block Brandon spotted their first mark. "Okay, see up there? Those two kids dressed like Ninja Turtles? You're gonna learn something tonight," he said, easing up on the accelerator. The golf cart slowed to a crawl just behind the Ninja Turtle kids. "Alright, when I give the signal, you're gonna jump out, grab their sacks, get back in, and we'll take off. Got it?"

"Why do I gotta do all the work? You jump out!" said Brice.

"Because I'm driving! You want candy, or you gonna puss out?"

"Alright! But we're switchin' later, because this is some serious bullshit. You always drive."

"Yeah, yeah... we'll switch later," said Brandon, lying. He took his foot off the accelerator and the golf cart rolled to a stop. "Okay, go!" Brice lumbered out and with all the stealth of a bull in a China shop, he trudged up behind the kids dressed as turtles. The one dressed as Leonardo turned around. "Oh my god! Look, it's Trump! Cool costume, bro!" The other dressed as Donatello turned too, lit up, and pointed. "Aww, check out their golf cart! Bro! That's sweet as hell!" he said. A few other trick-or-treaters noticed the golf cart too, and some began to chant, "USA! USA!" while others simply walked by, averting their gaze.

"What're you waitin' for, dumbass? Grab 'em!" said Brandon, beeping the horn. He tapped on the accelerator and the golf cart crawled forward.

"I'm here to make Halloween great again, bitches!" said Brice.

"Cool!" said the turtles in unison.

"Yeah... great for me!" said Brice. He lunged forward, grabbed their sacks, shoved them out of the way, then ran back into the street in pursuit of the sluggishly rolling golf cart.

"Slow down, asshole!" shouted Brice, running as fast as he could. Brandon eased up and slowed to a crawl and Brice attempted to hop in, but he lost his footing, tripped, and faceplanted onto the pavement. The sacks flew from his grasp, burst open, and candy scattered all over the street. Brandon stopped the cart as Brice, with the effort of a mortally wounded linebacker, got back onto his feet. Dazed, he hesitated, not really sure about what to do next. He turned to Brandon sitting in the driver's seat.

"Get in, dumbass! You can't do anything right, you know that?" said Brandon. Brice plopped hard onto the passenger seat. Brandon stepped on it and the golf cart sped off, while the Ninja Turtles stood on the sidewalk, mouths agape, their two hours of trick-or-treating all for naught. Leonardo looked at his friend and said, "Well, at least they're making Halloween great again."

"Yeah, for themselves," replied Donatello.

"You asshole! Why'd you take off on me like that?" said Brice, his hand grasping the oh-shit handle in a death grip. Brandon stomped on the accelerator and the golf cart responded, flags flapping proudly.

"Seriously, bro. It's so embarrassing being your twin sometimes, you know that?"

"It's all your fault! You sped off and I couldn't get in."

"Dude, I was going like two!" Brice was having the worst Halloween of his entire life and couldn't take it anymore. He let go of the oh-shit handle, pivoted for optimal vantage, raised his right arm, swung, and bitch-slapped Brandon hard across the face. Brandon's arms jerked counterclockwise and the speeding golf cart lurched violently, tilted upward onto its two right wheels, then smashed head-on into the fascia of a Cybertruck parked on the opposite side of the street. The twins catapulted from their seats, launched over the windshield, and belly-flopped onto the hood of the Tesla, then rolled off on opposite sides of the vehicle, Brandon plonking onto the grass, and Brice faceplanting hard onto the pavement for the second time in as many minutes. Brandon got up and dusted himself off while Brice lay on the pavement rolling and groaning. Chants of "USA! USA!" redoubled up and down the street.

Brandon noticed his blonde wig and MAGA cap laying on the hood of the Cybertruck. He grabbed the wig and cap and screwed them back onto top of his head. He walked around the golf cart and took in the damage. The front end had taken on the characteristics of an accordion, and the tires had been impaled and flattened by shards of fiberglass – the golf cart was an irreparable wreck. Brice's head popped up on the street side of the Cybertruck.

"Bro, what're we gonna do? Dad's golf cart is totaled! We're so dead," said Brice.

"No we're not. When's the last time we got in trouble – for anything? Stop being such a bitch and man up!" said Brandon. Brice wheezed through his open mouth as he thought about what Brandon had just said.

"You're right! We never get in trouble."

"We make trouble. Remember that," said Brandon, walking toward Brice.

"Okay, but this sucks because now we gotta walk. Maybe if you woulda let me drive – " Now it was Brandon who lost it. He raised his arm and swung, backhanding Brice hard across his tubby cheek. Brice took the full brunt of the slap and stumbled sideways.

"Nobody's driving it now, so get over it!" said Brandon. Brice couldn't remember when he'd been punched, hit, pummeled, smacked, and thrown so much. He decided to allow Brandon to continue calling the shots... for now. *But like Dad always says,* he thought, *payback's a bitch.*

"Okay, okay!" said Brice, rubbing his raw cheek. "But what're we gonna do? The golf cart is – "

"Just leave it! We'll tell Dad that someone musta stole it," said Brandon. They abandoned the wreck and walked off down Minden toward Crown Street, which would take them to the park.

"Hey! We can tell him it must've been the illegals!" said Brice.

"Now yer talkin'!"

7

"There you are!" said Finn, limping down Birkhill Street toward the park. "Where have you been?" By now most of the trick-or-treaters had made their ways back home to inspect and enjoy their bounties of candy, and parents girded themselves for the onslaught of the dreaded, late-night sugar high.

"Following, fooling, feeding. What else?" replied his shadowy, shimmery Friend, slithering up the trunk of a tree, then jumping into the canopy of the next. It wound down the trunk of yet another tree then joined Finn on the sidewalk toward the park. It sensed Finn's pain and spied bruises behind the burlap and with a flick of its upraised fingertip, Finn's injuries dissipated to a dark ectoplasm that vapored off his body. Finn's Friend inhaled swiftly, and the ectoplasm was sucked into the many holes in its head.

"Thank you," said Finn, his gait now strong, *sans* limp. These interventions had another effect: They prolonged Finn's life... but they also kept him from growing into an adult, locking him in a state of perpetual adolescence.

"I fed on disease tonight, but still I hunger. An old clown he was, and not long for this world. I found in him bad things and these I took."

"You must be talking about Mr. Marsh," said Finn. "He's a good guy. I'm glad you made him better."

"Yes. A Lazarus I performed upon him. He had to die to live, but now all is good. He'll rise again much, much better, oh yes, he will, much, much better." said Finn's Friend. Finn thought about how the night was progressing, and the many changes yet to take place.

"I told you they were mean, didn't I?" said Finn, cutting to the chase. "Viciously so."

"Oh yes! Spirited they are! And plump too," replied his shadowy Friend, smiling. His purplish tongue licking many rows of teeth in anticipation of the feast that lie ahead. He inhaled deeply through his holes and caught the stray whiff of a pumpkin spice candle that flickered inside a jack-o-lantern that sat atop a ladder just ahead. With a flick and a nod, the offending jack-o-lantern exploded in a shower of fiery sparks.

"That stench so offends!"

"I like it!" replied Finn.

"Ugh!" They walked along in silence taking in the evening. An old neighborhood this was, with a fine mix of large and small homes. Tudor and Federalist styles predominated, with a smattering of smaller Arts and Crafts, and Dutch Colonials, their stately gambrel roofs, and gabled windows reflecting the swift and solitary clouds above. And glorious trees! Elms, oaks, maples and beech, their branches crossing and mingling, forming a woody tunnel over the street.

"It's a pretty place, no?" asked Finn.

"Yes. And I rather feel we're doing it a favor."

"A big one, yes." Two costumed stragglers approached, out for those last treats, or perhaps a bit of devilry.

"Yo, cool costumes, bros! What're you supposed to be?" asked the one dressed like Jack Skellington.

"I'm a scarecrow," said Finn.

"Obviously," replied the other dressed as Beetlejuice. "But what are you?"

"He's a changeling," said Finn, "and my familiar," speaking on behalf of his Friend.

"Cool!" said the stragglers in unison. Finn's Friend hissed out a loud whistle, and steam ejaculated through the many holes in its head, as they passed.

"Woah! What the fuck?!" said Jack Skellington, jumping backward.

"That was totally bad-ass!" said Beetlejuice, laughing.

"They enjoyed that," said Finn, the stragglers receding off into the dark, chattering enthusiastically at what they'd just witnessed.

"How long this, our arrangement of mutual convenience? Remind one," said Finn's Friend.

"Next year will be two-hundred-and-fifty years," said Finn.

"My-my."

"Hey-hey!"

"What?"

"Never mind," said Finn. "It gets lonely."

"We can never stay long. We must detach."

"I know," said Finn. "Still, it isn't easy. Always moving from this place to that."

"We do what we do," said Finn's Friend.

"I know. But I think about those days sometimes, in the long, long ago — "

"Don't."

"Not very often," said Finn. "But tonight is hard."

"It's all so exhausting, but I so like this night above all nights, oh yes I do" said Finn's Friend.

"And here we are," said Finn.

"Yessss," hissed Finn's Friend. The concrete sidewalk turned into an aggregate path as they walked through the arched entrance, ignoring the *Park Closed After Dark* sign. Off to the left, a child-enticing playground with swing sets, a tall chrome slide, and a colorful jungle gym that resembled a pirate ship. To the right, a forested area with towering trees. Further still, a grassy area with grills and picnic tables, a baseball diamond, tennis courts, and a soccer field.

"There it is," said Finn, pointing out a lone, ancient, and towering oak that stood on a mound.

"Perfect," said Finn's Friend. "I'll prepare, then off I go. More tricks and loose strings to tie."

8

Logan didn't know what to do, and even though he could have walked these streets blindfolded, he felt utterly lost. He passed by jack-o-lanterns glowing on porches, their toothy smiles laughing at and mocking him. Up ahead on a lawn, two giant skeletons, one holding an axe cocked high and readied to strike, the other crouched on all fours, its neck resting on a chopping block. Logan walked by the impressive skeletal display numb, with nary a glance.

He spied costumed children through picture windows kneeling on floors, organizing their bounty of candy while their parents looked on contentedly. Hot, bitter tears streamed down his cheeks while he imagined that little girl in the bumblebee costume organizing her candy while that guy and his very pregnant mom sat on the couch looking on blissfully... smiling, laughing, and having a great time while he walked alone and forgotten. It was late and he seemed to be the only trick-or-treater left on these now, somehow unfamiliar, tree-lined streets where he was nothing more than a stranger. Someone to be chased off. Laughed at. Forgotten.

He couldn't, nor would he go to Brandon and Brice's house, even if it was the last house on Earth. *Fuck them, forever*, he thought. He thought about going to Kevin's but then he remembered they have cats, and he's deathly allergic, and that only reminded him that he didn't have his inhaler. What will he do if he has an attack? *I guess I'll just die*, he thought. *Then I can be with Dad.* The tears started again.

It had been a while since he'd thought of Dad, who was killed when his Army chopper went down in a training exercise accident. There's a framed picture of Dad and a four-year-old Logan on Mom's dresser; Dad in his flight suit holding Logan's hand, and Logan wearing Dad's huge flight helmet with the chopper behind them—the one that crashed. And it wasn't

Dad's fault. One of the mechanics forgot to check something and six soldiers died that day, all because of some stupid mistake. Mom had hung Dad's memorial box on Logan's bedroom wall; the box held Dad's tri-folded flag, his medals, awards, and rank insignias.

"Hey Dad? It's me, Logan," he said through tears. "I miss you so much and I wish you were here. I don't know what's going on, and I'm so lost, and Mom doesn't even know me anymore, and it's like I don't even exist. I don't know what I'm gonna do and I need your help. Can you hear me? Dad?" Logan stopped walking under the canopy of a huge oak tree, buried his face in his hands and wept. "I can't take this, Dad. Please help me. I don't know what I'm gonna do. I'm so lost." Logan heard a snap high in the tree above, and a small branch struck the sidewalk at his feet. He looked up and saw it, the thing, dark and sparkly, looking down at him. *It's that thing I saw at Brandon and Brice's,* he thought. And there it was, perched on a high up branch with its arm hooked around the trunk. Logan wasn't even scared. At least he wasn't alone anymore.

"What do you want?" he shouted up at it. The thing coiled around the trunk and looped downward, like stripes on a barber pole, and now it stood on a branch about ten feet directly above Logan. "That's a pretty cool costume," said Logan. "Who are you? Are you Finn's Friend? Would you tell him I'm sorry... please?" Then in a blur it shot off into the next tree, then into the next tree after that, and it was so quick it hardly registered. The only thing that allowed Logan to keep track of it was how it sparkled. It was so black... Vantablack, but its sparkles gave it away, like a constellation of stars on a pitch-black night... a night like tonight.

"Don't be scared," Logan shouted. "I won't hurt you." And then something extraordinary happened. Up ahead at the corner of Crown and Minden, a man in a flight suit walked out from behind a tree, then he turned away and began to walk down Crown toward the park. If this was a joke it was a really cruel one, but Logan had to find out.

"Hey, Dad! Wait up!" Logan's heart was hammering in his chest as the surge of adrenaline flooded his bloodstream. He took off and mad-dashed it toward the man in the flight suit, but no matter how fast he ran, the man could not be caught.

"Dad! Hold-up, wait for me!" But the man kept walking, his pace steady and confident. *That is my dad, right?* thought Logan. *It's gotta be.* But Logan could not catch up, which didn't make any sense because he was running three times as fast as the man was walking, but if anything, the distance between them only increased.

And then Logan remembered the twins and the plans they'd had for Finn. He wasn't sure if the plans were still in play due to Halloween basically falling apart from the moment they'd set off, but he knew how mean Brandon and Brice could be, and just because he was no longer involved didn't mean that they weren't going to carry out their plan. *I've got to get to the park,* he thought. *Finn's dead if those two get ahold of him.* Logan noticed the distance between him and his dad diminishing... he was finally catching up. "Wait up, Dad!" shouted Logan. And now he was only a few paces behind. Logan's dad kept up his steady pace, but then he turned around, smiled, and nodded his head in a gesture of encouragement. Logan took it as a sign: *Come on son... you've got this.* Logan finally caught up, and Dad put his hand on Logan's back and gently prodded him on toward the park entrance.

The concrete sidewalk turned into an aggregate path as he walked through the arched entrance, ignoring the *Park Closed After Dark* sign. Up ahead he saw something very strange, and very out of place in this place that he knew so well: a tree that had been stripped of its branches and bark, with the branches arranged in a spiral around the bare trunk. At the entrance of the spiral stood Finn. Something wasn't right and Logan stopped, suddenly afraid. He turned to Dad for guidance... but Dad was gone.

9

Brandon and Brice sat on the bleachers at Kimball Middle School's baseball diamond looking through the sacks of candy they'd confiscated from the two Mexican kids in the *Dia de los Muertos* costumes. They had also confiscated their sombreros, giving their Trump costumes a very ironic twist. Brice opened the sack he'd taken from the smaller one and held it open for Brandon.

"See? I told you they were stealing from American trick-or-treaters. Look how much more candy's in this one!"

"Yep. They should have the same amount," said Brandon, tearing into his fifth Reese's peanut butter cup. Piles of wrappers lay crumpled at their feet. "It only makes sense. And bro, the night's not over. We still gotta find Finn." Brandon stood and hoisted the sack of candy over his shoulder, like a hunter with his bounty of game.

"I got my second wind. Let's go," said Brandon.

"We could totally be ICE agents!" said Brice standing.

"That's the dream. It's gonna happen!" Brandon stepped off the bleacher and headed toward the sidewalk, Brice a few paces behind.

"Right? Oh, and bro? The way you body slammed that taller Mexican kid to the ground? Like a total boss!" said Brice.

"And the way you arm-locked the little one!" said Brandon

"He tried getting away, but not on my watch," said Brice.

They had happened upon the *dia de los muertos* boys when they'd turned the corner of Crown Street and Flanders, a few minutes after trying to steal the candy from the kids dressed as the Ninja Turtles, just before destroying their father's golf cart. They had been walking along and bumped into the Mexican kids a few blocks from the park. They'd turned the corner and BOOM! There they were.

"When Dad hears about what we did, he won't even care about the golf cart," said Brandon. They exited the school grounds and headed east on Flanders.

"I know! And did you hear the snap when I jerked his arm?"

"Bro! I knew right there and then that you'd broken it. You totally redeemed yourself tonight," said Brandon, raising his palm. They high-fived.

"Thanks, bro." Up ahead, two giant skeletons, one with an axe held high, cocked and readied to strike, and the other down on all fours, its neck resting on a chopping block. "Woah," said the twins in unison. "That's bad-ass!" They continued on toward the park, leaving a trail of candy wrappers in their wake.

"I don't know if we should be wearing these things," said Brandon. He removed the sombrero from his head, revealing the MAGA cap, but within the span of five steps it became too annoying to hold the sack of candy in one hand and the sombrero in the other.

"I know. They're good souvenirs though," said Brice, fingering the brim of the stolen sombrero.

"Are they? Seriously bro, I can't even look at this thing anymore," said Brandon. He chucked the sombrero Frisbee style and it sailed off into the dark onto someone's lawn. "*Sayonara*, you piece of shit!"

"What?" asked Brice.

"That's Mexican for SEE YA."

"Seriously bro, how do you know so much?"

"You know in the car how Dad always says shut up and listen when he's got talk radio on? That's what I do. I shut up and listen."

"I try but that shit's so boring. I can't even."

"Well, you asked. That's why I'm so smart. I shut up and listen."

"Well, I'm keepin' my sombrero as a souvenir," said Brice.

"Yeah but you gotta take it off, bro. It's embarrassing walking next to you wearing that thing," said Brandon, then he reached up and yanked it from Brice's head, but the blonde wig and MAGA cap snagged and slid off, dropping to the sidewalk.

"Asshole! Give it back!" said Brice, snatching the wig and cap off the sidewalk, but he stumbled and found himself down on all fours. Brandon held the sombrero high, cocked and readied it, then wound up like a pitcher standing at the mound. He hurled it and off it spun, sailing high into a tree.

"Haw-haw! Kiss your souvenir g'bye," said Brandon.

"You're an asshole!" said Brice, looking up at the sombrero stuck in the tree.

"Why you so triggered?"

"I ain't triggered. Seriously bro, why you gotta fuck with me like that?"

"Just drop it... I'm warning you," said Brandon. The sugar was beginning to spike and the sweat under his hot wig was making him itchy, and he could feel the arteries throbbing in his neck.

"Whatever, dude," said Brice. He stormed ahead to put a little distance between himself and his unpredictable twin brother."

"I'm just messin' with ya, bro!" shouted Brandon. "Don't take it so serious!" On they walked, Brice a few steps ahead. It was dark and the night was cool. After a couple of blocks of stewing in silence, their tempers eased, and a détente of sorts took hold. The concrete sidewalk turned into an aggregate path as they walked through the arched entrance, ignoring the *Park Closed After Dark* sign, but what they saw just ahead turned their faces ashen.

"DUDE!"

"NO WAY!"

A lone tree in the field had been stripped of its branches and bark, and the branches had been arranged in a spiral around the bare trunk. At the entrance of the spiral sparkled Finn.

10

Logan took a deep breath and screwed up his courage. His mouth was dry and the cut inside his cheek had started to scab over, staunching most of the bleeding. He took his first tentative steps deeper into the park, and was now face to face with Finn.

"Hey," said Logan.

"Hey back," said Finn.

"I um... I was really mean to you earlier, and... I'm really sorry. I was a real jerk. Sorry," said Logan, his hands buried deep into his pockets and his head bowed in shame.

"That's okay," said Finn.

"No it's not," said Logan.

"I think we're all having a pretty crappy night," said Finn.

"You're not kidding," said Logan. "This has been the worst night of my entire life... bar none, and I've got no one but myself to blame," said Logan.

"There's always next year," said Finn.

"No way! I'm never going trick-or-treating again as long as I live. I'm done," said Logan.

"Then let's get outta here. Come on... I'll walk you home." Finn reached out and put his hand on Logan's shoulder, and Logan realized this was the second time that someone had reached out in kindness toward him.

"Come on," said Finn, "Let's go." They both turned and began their walk back toward the park entrance.

"You're not gonna believe me, but so many weird things happened tonight that don't make any sense," said Logan. They walked out of the park under the arched entrance. Finn could tell that something was definitely not right with his new friend. He saw someone who seemed completely lost and rudderless. It was a little heartbreaking... but it was also part of the process. They came upon a bus stop with a bench. Logan stopped, sat, and buried his face into his palms.

"What's the matter?" asked Finn, looking at Logan sitting there in the midst of a panic attack. He sat next to Logan. "Don't you want to go home?" Logan looked at Finn, then away as a fresh, black mascara tear tracked down his cheek.

"I went home earlier, and my mom didn't know me anymore, like I was a complete stranger. And she was pregnant! My mom wasn't pregnant when I left! And there was some strange guy and his little girl living with her," said Logan. "I know you probably think I'm crazy, but it's true! All of it! And then after, when I was walking I saw this... thing, I don't know what, all black and sparkly, and then all the sudden my dad appeared out of nowhere, and that's crazy, because my dad died five years ago! It doesn't make any sense! Nothing makes any sense! And here I am going crazy. Seriously! What's wrong with me?"

"There's nothing wrong with you," said Finn. You're just having the worst night of your life."

Logan cupped his face into his hands and rocked back and forth. "I don't know what I'm going to do," he said.

"I do," said Finn, standing. "You're gonna get up with me and we're gonna walk back to your home, and everything will be fine, I promise." Logan, crushed under the weight of everything that had happened since he'd left his mom earlier that evening, was now angry.

"How can you say that? You have no idea what I've been through!" said Logan.

"Yes I do," said Finn. "You just told me. Now come on, let's go. And I promise you, everything will be fine... you'll see."

11

Brandon and Brice looked at each other and smiled in anticipation of the imminent slaughter, then commenced their walk toward Finn and the mangled tree.

"Kinda weird how that tree is destroyed just like ours," said Brice.

"Now we know who did it, and it's payback time," said Brandon. He dropped the sack of candy he'd stolen and rubbed his small hands together. Brice dropped his sack too, then cracked his knuckles.

"Hey there, Finn! Long time, no see," said Brice. "Time for round two!"

"And I'm not missing out this time," said Brandon. "Ready or not, here we come!"

Finn stood silently at the entrance of the spiral in his scarecrow outfit. Brice noticed flashes and sparkles strobing from under the tatters of Finn's costume. Brandon noticed them too, but it was just another weird thing on a long list of weird things about the new kid. *This is gonna be fun,* he thought. Then Finn turned and disappeared into the spiral. The twins followed.

"You can run, but you can't hide!" said Brandon.

Neither of them could possibly have known that they had just stepped into a powerfully charmed spiral, and the further they ventured, the stranger things became. The branches piled on either side transformed to solid, shiny, iridescent walls that curved ever inward in swirls of color, like the interior of a conch shell, leading them deeper and deeper, and the spiral went on and on. Perspectives shifted and right-left-up-down rules no longer applied. The hall became a tube that turned and pulsed, lapping in on itself in four dimensions and Finn sparkled ahead, always just out of reach. Time folded and doubled back, and a stream of memories flickered in and out of consciousness: a plywood ramp and bicycle crash, Dad drunk, snapping his belt, scrolling porn under the covers at 2 a.m., splooshing down a cool-blue waterslide, watching Dad and Mom through the slats of the closet door, the principal's red, angry face, the gold fish gasping on the carpet, picking a scab off a knee, a big, red D- in math, laughing at a cartoon, giving Jacob a bloody nose at recess, ripping the parakeet's wing off, biting the dentist, ramming a twig into Brice's nose as he slept, French fries slathered with catsup, making Emily touch it.

Brandon looked down, around, and up as the sun arched across the sky with blinding speed, but then it was dark and the moon shot from out of the horizon faster than a shooting star, again, and again, and again. Brice wondered why Brandon looked so much younger, then he turned and saw multiple images of himself reflecting off the walls, and why did he look seven... or was he six? Hard to tell, but now he looked four. They flopped and tumbled out of their giant costumes, leaving a trail of clothes behind.

Practicing the letter K, frying a grasshopper with a magnifying glass, sucking a Capri Sun through a straw, cramming colorful, plastic shapes into the correct holes, locked and angry in the baby seat, a burning rash, a burp and eruption of vomit, the excruciating pain of circumcision, and all these memories and traumas, these atrocities, and horrors were drawn and exorcised from the twins that swirled in a cacophony of ectoplasmic dervishes that whirled directly into the holes of Finn's Friend.

Brandon saw Brice and giggled at his bald toddler twin who looked back at him and giggled. They collapsed onto their knees and crawled toward the sparkles on all fours, and now they sat facing each other, two naked babies, pattycake laughing and cooing, their chubby arms and legs flexing in joyful tandem.

"Ma-ma-ma," said baby Brandon.

"Ga-ga-ga," said baby Brice.

"Ma-ma."

"Ga-ga."

"Ma-Ga."

Finn's Friend morphed back into its Vantablack form, its disguise no longer necessary. It bent down and picked the babies up and carried them even further into the spiral where the further he went, the younger they got. The spiral terminated at the trunk of the tree. Finn's Friend gently placed the newborn infants between woody folds of the trunk where they safely cradled. They squirmed, herky-jerky, their peanut bodies wrinkled, pink, and prune-like, their umbilical cords tied, and amniotic fluid glistening on their skin. Finn's Friend crouched and tenderly caressed the infant's cheeks and both fell quickly into a deep sleep. Finn's Friend cupped its hands together and two small orbs of bright light ascended from out of its upturned palms where they hovered in the air just above the infants. Then its shiny, black fingertips pointed at each infant, guiding the orbs downward. The orbs descended onto the chest of each infant where they rested for a moment before they were absorbed deep into each infant's heart. The infants lit up momentarily in a warm glow revealing skeletons, networks of veins, arteries, and nerves, then they dimmed into two perfect and beautiful infant boys sleeping soundly in the folds of the tree trunk.

Finn's Friend stood from its crouch, looked down at the infants one last time, then latched onto the trunk and spiraled upward to the very tip. It raised its arms heavenward and the swiftly moving clouds slowed. It spun its hands and fingertips in an intricate choreography, and the clouds above slowly spun clockwise and downward in a vortex toward the tip of the bare tree, faster and faster still. The wind picked up and the park's trees swayed and groaned, their autumn-colored leaves flying off in clockwise eddies and swirls.

Finn's Friend raised its outspread arms, clenched its fists, then slammed them together like a hammer striking an anvil, and a bolt of lightning flashed from the vortex above and struck the bare tree igniting both it and the spiraled branches in a fiery inferno. The tree and spiral exploded with flames flickering and dancing a hundred feet into the air, and the park glowed eerily in alternating shades of oranges, reds, purples, and yellows.

A mile from the park, Brandon and Brice shot out and tumbled from the spiral of branches on their front lawn, emerging once again as the teenagers they were when their bizarre Halloween had begun hours earlier. Finn's Friend stood there, undisguised and Vantablack. Whisps of smoke and steam curled from out of its holes, and its sparkles flashed and blinked. The boys stared spellbound at the strange figure, but then it pointed in the direction of the park. Brandon and Brice turned and looked at the sky above the park glowing and winking, with the occasional far-off flame licking violently above the horizon of rooftops and the autumn-tinted foliage. In his own way, each boy realized that he was witnessing a bonfire of his past wickedness, an inferno of his many transgressions, misdeeds, violence, and depravities. It left each boy feeling exposed, stripped, and utterly vulnerable, and for the first time in their lives they knew remorse. A cold wind blew in, and with it a hint of the impending winter that lay ahead.

Brandon and Brice turned in tandem back toward Finn's Friend... for what? An answer? Guidance? But it was gone. They hadn't noticed that it had twisted its way toward the top of their tree which had been miraculously made whole again—every branch firmly attached, from trunk to tip. Finn's Friend now perched at the top of the tree. It shifted its gaze from the boys standing below and scanned the horizon.

In a twinkling flash, it shot off to find Finn.

The porch light snapped on and the front door opened.

"What the hells-the-matter with you two, standing there naked as jaybirds?!" shouted Dad. "Get in here before you get arrested!" Brandon and Brice looked at each other, shell-shocked, like two soldiers staggering off a battlefield. They ascended the porch steps, walked through the door and into their home.

"I don't know what I'm gonna do if she chases me off again," said Logan.

"It was a weird night for sure, but I think everything's gonna be okay," said Finn. He looked up and a smile creased his face, having noticed his Friend sparkling high in the canopy of a giant sycamore just up the street, but there was a deep sorrow attached to this smile of Finn's. He wished more than anything that he could stay, and that Logan and he could become best friends.

"I really think it's gonna be okay," said Finn. Logan thought he heard something catch in Finn's voice and he looked at him.

"I gotta admit it, Finn. Your costume really freaked me out when I first saw you at Brandon and Brice's," said Logan.

"Really?" Logan put his hand on Finn's shoulder as they walked side by side.

"Oh, yeah," said Logan, with a chuckle. "You really got me good!"

It was well past midnight, and the hundreds of trick-or-treaters that had swarmed the streets hours earlier were safely tucked into their beds, most fast asleep, but others wide awake, having eaten too much of their candy.

They turned the corner of Logan's street and walked on. Porches were dark as were the jack-o-lanterns, their candles long since winking out in undulating curls of smoke. One porch just ahead was brightly lit, with someone nervously pacing its length, her wristwatch indicating that it was well past midnight. She looked up, turned and saw her son approaching, still in his Count Dracula costume. She could tell that he'd been crying for all the tears that had tracked through the make-up on his face.

"LOGAN!" she shouted, bounding off the porch and running toward him. "Where have you been? I've been worried sick!"

"Mom?" said Logan. "You know me? You know who I am?" She grabbed him by the shoulders, then pulled him into her so tightly he nearly lost his breath. Logan wrapped his arms around his mom and buried his face into her shoulder and began to weep all over again.

"What's the matter with you? You're my son and I love you more than anything on this Earth, and don't you forget it, but you've got some explaining to do," she said, as they turned and walked toward their home. Logan turned around to thank Finn for being such a great friend in his hour of need. But Finn was gone.

EPILOGUE

It had been a month since the worst night of Logan's entire life. That was one Halloween that he kept trying to put behind him, but bad dreams and stress had plagued many of his nights since, and he'd been having trouble sleeping. The stitches in his cheek had been removed two days earlier, and he traced the bumpy scar with his tongue.

It was a brisk and chilly Saturday afternoon, typical for late November, and Logan lay in bed with his head propped on a stack of pillows. He looked at his dad's display case hanging on the wall above his desk; the tri-fold flag, his many medals, and rank insignias. Dad was about to be promoted to major when he was killed. He remembered his dad coming home from combat and spending a lot of time shut in the bedroom. He'd asked Mom why Dad was so sad, and she had said something about Post Traumatic Stress Disorder, but that Dad was strong and was getting better. Logan worried that he was suffering from something similar.

He heard the doorbell ring and his mom's steps. A minute later she knocked on his bedroom door.

He got up and opened it.

"Hey. Brandon and Brice are at the door," she said. "Should I tell them you're busy?" Logan thought about it for a second.

"No. Lemme see what they want," he replied. Now pensive, Mom bit her lip as Logan walked out of his room toward the front door. She knew that this was something he'd have to handle on his own.

Logan put his jacket on then walked out onto the porch where Brandon and Brice were waiting.

They had lost quite a bit of weight and were looking a lot more fit than they had on Halloween.

"Hey... gotta be honest, guys. I'm not exactly thrilled to see either of you." said Logan. Brandon and Brice rocked and shifted uncomfortably, their hands buried deep into their pockets.

"I totally get that," said Brandon.

"So do I," said Brice. "We've been grounded for the last month, and today's the first day we've been allowed out."

"It's true," said Brandon.

"So why're you guys here?" asked Logan.

"To say sorry," said Brandon.

"I'm sorry too," said Brice. "For everything."

"Me too," said Brandon. "I'm so sorry for pushing you and punching you." Logan was skeptical and even a little suspicious, thinking that at any minute their veneer of regret would crack, and they'd transform into the bullies they were on Halloween... but it never happened. *Are these guys being for real?* he thought.

"Are your parents making you do this," asked Logan.

"No," they replied in unison.

"They don't even know we're here," said Brandon. Logan also had no way of knowing that Brandon and Brice's next stop would be to visit Miguel and Carlos, the *Dia de los Muertos* boys at their home, where their apologies would be met with a similar volume of skepticism... but bruises, fractures, and cuts require a time of healing.

The next day Mom had a few errands to run and Logan was bored, so he decided to tag along. Mom put the Chevy into reverse and pulled out of the driveway. She drove up the street and turned left on Birkhill. Up ahead Logan saw Brandon and Brice raking leaves at Mr. Marsh's — where Brandon had shoved Logan into his bushes, ruining them. Mr. Marsh was out on his lawn too, bagging leaves.

"Hey Mom, would you mind if I got out here?" asked Logan.

"Not at all," she replied. "What's up?" Mom pulled to the curb in front of Mr. Marsh's house, stopped and looked at Logan as he unbuckled.

"I'm just gonna help rake some leaves."

Acknowledgements

Andrew Lark

It took the time and talent of many people to help this collection of short stories come to fruition, and I owe a deep depth of gratitude to the following people: Pam Malane, Gregory Miller, Andy Lockwood, Sara Wolf-Molnar, and Susan Muller, all of whom read earlier drafts of "Finn's Friend" and "Dread Box" and offered their helpful and valuable feedback. Thank you Nancy Arnfield, Suzanne Allen, and Robert Quandt for allowing me the use of ink wells, skulls, candles, various antiques, textiles, and other objects of the occult for the cover photograph. A big, giant thank you to Virginia Lark Moyer for her keen eye and deft editing. You make my words sing! Thanks again to Sara Wolf-Molnar for taking the time out of your incredibly busy schedule to write your brilliant forward. I look forward to further collaborations with you! Thanks also to Donald Levin, my fellow author, for participating in *The Devil's Quill* and writing his two great Halloween stories, brilliantly incorporating Jewish mythology tropes into this collection. Thank you Paddy Lynch, owner of the Detroit Convent in Hamtramck, Michigan, and Eric and Candice Law, owners of the Color | Ink Studio in Hazel Park, Michigan, for their generosity in hosting our book launch events at their incredible facilities. Thanks to Ziggy, our Golden Jack Terrier for reminding me that long walks and tummy rubs are an important part of the process. And lastly, a huge thank you to my wife Karen, for her never-ending encouragement and patience while I typed, revised, and edited from morning till night until this, *The Devil's Quill,* became ready for you, dear reader, to enjoy and give you the requisite chills that will keep you awake deep into the night. I work very hard on my stories, and it means a lot to me that you purchased this book. I sincerely hope you enjoy it, cover to cover. Thank you very much!

Donald Levin

My great thanks to my friend and fellow author Andrew Charles Lark for conceiving of this project and inviting me into it. Warm thanks to Virginia Lark Moyer for her close editing. I also wish to acknowledge the 1937 Yiddish language Polish film *Der Dibuk* directed by Michał Waszyński and based on the play *The Dybbuk* by S. Ansky. This film provided the basis for the tale that Sarah Friedman tells in "The Curse of the Dybbuk." I particularly wish to thank my wife Suzanne Allen for her constant love and support.

If you enjoyed reading this book, please consider posting a review on Amazon, Goodreads, and/or the individual author's websites.

About the Authors

Andrew Lark

Andrew Charles Lark has written many short stories and plays. He's also written *Dark Waters*, a five-episode horror podcast, and a novel, *Better Boxed and Forgotten*. His play, *Stop Up Your Ears!* is a recipient of Wayne State University's Heck-Rabi award for playwrighting. Another play, *Ask Me! Tell Me!* was professionally produced at both the Ringwald Theatre's GPS play festival in Ferndale, Michigan, and The Hudson Theatre's Play by Play Festival in Hudson, New York, where it won a Ten Best award. Andrew Lark has also collaborated previously with Donald Levin and Wendy Sura Thomson on a dystopian trilogy, *Postcards From the Future: A Triptych on Humanity's End*—three short stories that address the end of humanity. Andrew has many other writing projects pending, including new plays, new episodes of *Dark Waters*, an illustrated children's book, and another novel. Stay tuned....

Donald Levin

Donald Levin is an award-winning fiction writer and poet. He is the author of *Savage City*, a historical novel set in 1932 Detroit, *The Arsenal of Deceit*, a historical novel set in 1941, and *The Ghosts of Detroit*, a historical novel set in 1955; seven Martin Preuss mystery novels; and *The House of Grins* (Poison Toe Press, 2025), a novel; three books of poetry, *Are You Listening* (West Vine Press, 2024), *In Praise of Old Photographs* (Little Poem Press, 2005), and *New Year's Tangerine* (Pudding House Press, 2007); *The Exile* (Poison Toe Press, 2020), a dystopian novella; and co-author with Andrew Charles Lark and Wendy Thomson of *Postcards from the Future: A Triptych on Humanity's End* (Whistlebox Press and Quitt and Quinn Publishers, 2019). He lives in Ferndale, Michigan. To learn more about Donald and his works, visit his website, www.donaldlevin.com, and follow him on Instagram @donald_levin_author.

Also by these Authors

Andrew Charles Lark

Better Boxed and Forgotten: A horror and suspense novel about a man who inherits the family mansion and discovers his great-grandfather's meticulously archived treasure trove of forgotten papers, secret military hardware, and fantastic inventions, and one invention in particular with strange and fantastic powers that inadvertently opens doors with horrible and deadly consequences.

Postcards From The Future: A Triptych On Humanity's End, with co-authors, Donald Levin and Wendy Sura Thomson. A dystopian anthology with three stories: "Pollen" (Lark), "The Bright And Darkened Lands Of The Earth" (Levin), and "Silo Six" (Sura-Thomson). Each story imaginatively addresses a different take on the end of humanity.

Donald Levin

The Detroit Trilogy

Detroit, 1932. The fates of four people converge during a violent week of labor unrest in the bleakest year of the Great Depression. Against the backdrop of the bloody Ford Hunger March, events hurl these four into the center of a political storm that will change them—and their city—forever.

Detroit, 1941. With the nation on the brink of war, four people unite against the subversive forces that threaten Detroit, America's "arsenal of democracy." *The Arsenal of Deceit* recreates a rich historical period with chilling parallels to our own time.

Detroit, 1955. Factory closings. The Red Scare. Racial hatred. Four shattered characters take an unforgettable journey through these forces that shaped mid-century America.

The Martin Preuss Mystery Series

One cold November night, police detective Martin Preuss joins a frantic search for a seven-year-old girl with epilepsy who has disappeared from the streets of his suburban Detroit community. Probing deep into the anguished lives of all those who came into contact with the missing girl, Preuss must solve the many crimes of love he uncovers.

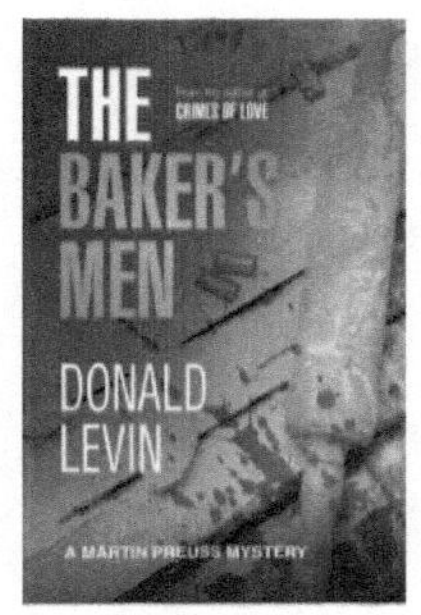

Easter, 2009. Ferndale Police detective Martin Preuss is spending a quiet evening with his son Toby when he's called out to investigate an after-hours shooting at a bakery in his suburban Detroit community. Struggling with the dizzying uncertainties of the case and hindered by the treachery of his own colleagues who scheme against him, Preuss is drawn into a whirlwind of greed and revenge spanning generations.

Preuss is called out to search for a van that has disappeared along with the woman who was driving and her passenger, a handicapped young man. Working through layer upon layer of secrets, Preuss exposes a multitude of contemporary crimes with roots in the twentieth century's darkest period.

When a friend asks newly retired detective Martin Preuss to look for a boy who disappeared forty years ago, the former investigator gradually becomes consumed with finding the forgotten child. Preuss revisits the countercultural fervor of Detroit in the 1970s—and plunges into hidden worlds of guilty secrets and dark crimes that won't stay buried.

Twenty years have passed since Raymond Douglas went to prison for the kidnapping and murder of a local businessman's wife. Now Douglas's daughter has hired private investigator Martin Preuss to track down a previously-unknown accomplice to the crime—who may or may not even exist.

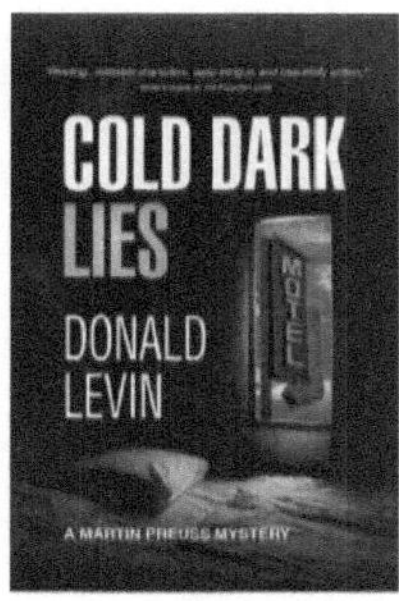

A young man takes a walk on the wild side and ends up clinging to life in a suburban Detroit motel. When private investigator Martin Preuss searches for the reason, he plunges into the young man's dark world of secrets and lies.

When the police investigation into the murder of a retired professor stalls, friends of the dead man plead with PI Martin Preuss to learn what happened. The twisting tale leads him across Detroit into a treacherous world of long-buried family secrets . . . where the painful relations between parents and children meet the deadly gathering storm of domestic terrorism.